MORE PRAISE FOR WILLIAM HJORTSBERG

"Re: *Gray Matters.* Chilling has to be the word. And more than that, superb writing."—Rod Sterling

"I don't remember seeing comic figments as extravagant as these, or as effective in this way. Hjortsberg burnishes every movement of this compact, lighting novel with language that is new and unstudied. I finish this book committed to read everything he writes."—Thomas McGuane, on *Alp*

"A satanic S. J. Perelman . . . by way of Disney and de Sade." —John Leonard, *The New York Times* on *Alp*

"Hjortsberg's first novel is full of surprises, the best of which is his clean-cool style and language. . . . Hjortsberg has it, the kind of alchemy which transmutes cow slop into gold." —Henri Ruggero, *Raleigh News and Observer,* on *Alp*

"*Alp* is that very rare thing, the solemnly promised bellylaugh which is delivered."—Richard Condon

"A novel full of surprise and invention. What strikes me as most impressive is the quality of Mr. Hjortsberg's imagination, which is on an order of Borges'. It is incredible to me how the man literally manufactures new worlds and makes them run as if several thousand years of tradition lay behind them. *Gray Matters* matters as a tour de force of novelistic invention."—Stanley Elkin

"*[Gray Matters]* raises nothing less than the question: What is the point of living? And Hjortsberg makes that question uproariously funny."—Digby Diehl, *The Los Angeles Times*

"All of it, from first page to last, is a pure joy to read. Hjortsberg has created a world of his own with such intense care and attention to detail that it becomes our world in the reading."—Harry Crews, *The New York Times Book Review* on *Gray Matters*

"Unforgettable characterizations. Hjortsberg has me hooked."
—*The Houston Post*, on *Gray Matters*

"He has pressed a weird poetry of science-fiction out of the jargon of the American space program and plunged us into a verbal experience as arresting as those final scenes of Stanley Kubrick's film, *2001. . . .*"—Christopher Lehmann-Haupt, *The New York Times* on *Toro! Toro! Toro!*

"The prose that propels these characters toward their just or excessive deserts is swift, clear, and efficient. . . The bravura dexterities of *Toro! Toro! Toro!* are enough to gladden the downest eyes, as the white light of all Hjortsberg's prose is enough to clear them."—George Stade, *The New York Times Book Review*

ODD CORNERS

The Slip-Stream World of William Hjortsberg

WILLIAM HJORTSBERG

SHOEMAKER & HOARD
Washington, DC

Library of Congress Cataloging-in-Publication Data is available.

ISBN 1-59376-021-3

Book design by Mark McGarry, Texas Type & Book Works
Set in Trump Mediaeval

Printed in the United States of America

Shoemaker & Hoard
A Division of Avalon Publishing Group, Inc.
Distributed by Publishers Group West

10 9 8 7 6 5 4 3 2 1

For Janie

CONTENTS

INTRODUCTION

"My God, he's committed science fiction." So wrote Harry Crews in 1971 in his review of *Gray Matters* for the *New York Times Book Review.* Of course, it helped that he went on to say the novel "turns out to be not SciFi, but an engrossing fiction informed by an imaginative use of science." Still, Crews had a point to make. Writers of serious literary fiction weren't supposed to dirty their lily-white hands with generic trash. It didn't matter that such fine work as *The Oxbow Incident* and *The Bronc People* were westerns, that both *1984* and *Brave New World* should be classified as science fiction, and that Dashiell Hammett and Raymond Chandler both wrote what anyone would define as detective *literature.* Genre fiction remained something one despised and avoided at all costs. Even the slightest exposure might infect a writer with a bad case of brow-lowering.

I just didn't get it. Anyone who reads for enjoyment (and

what other reason is there for opening a work of fiction?) knows not to risk such premature judgment. Otherwise, we all would have to give up on the manifold pleasures of Kurt Vonnegut, Graham Greene, Shirley Jackson, John le Carré and Stanislaw Lem, to mention but a few of the "serious" writers who have ventured into forbidden genre territory. I first encountered science fiction at a summer camp when I was twelve. Among the handful of battered secondhand books in the mess hall library was a first edition of Ray Bradbury's *The Martian Chronicles*, published three years earlier. From the opening blasts of "Rocket Summer" to the final loneliness of "There Shall Come Soft Rains" and "The Million-Year Picnic," I was spellbound. Before this, I had read only comic books, golden age cape-wearing superheros and the more disturbing psychosexual horrors of the EC canon. Bradbury introduced me to the joys of literature and he remains a favorite author to this day.

In high school, I devoured the work of Hemingway, Faulkner, Fitzgerald, Dos Passos, Thomas Wolfe and J. D. Salinger (who had also attended McBurney), but in many ways, my heart still belonged to Bradbury. Yet, when I first began writing fiction with a certain seriousness myself, my models were Hemingway and Salinger and not the cherished Ray. I knew well enough to avoid science fiction's curse. By my mid-twenties, I had written two fairly conventional novels that went nowhere (although the second earned me a Stegner Fellowship at Stanford), and when at twenty-seven

I found that the only job for which I qualified was as a stock boy in a grocery store, I realized I had ruined my life with the pursuit of literature.

Writers never choose to write. Rather they discover over time that, for better or worse, writing is in their nature. They simply can't help themselves. Although I had abandoned all hope of ever earning a living from my writing, I nevertheless continued to write. Every afternoon, when I returned home from a day of trimming lettuce and stamping prices on the tops of canned dog food, I'd sit down at my portable Royal and rattle off a page or two purely for my own pleasure. And here came the breakthrough failure had compelled me to confront. Because I no longer contemplated a writing career, I was free to abandon all the "rules" I had acquired preparing for it: always write what you know, write from experience, never write when stoned, keep a notebook handy. I gave up the misguided notion that writing is hard work. From now on, I wrote for the fun of it, for the sheer exuberant pleasure of making things up. I wrote when I was high as a kite. Best of all, I wrote what I didn't know.

The outcome of all this rule-breaking fooling around was *Alp*, a zany sex-farce set in a mythical Switzerland, work that led John Leonard to call me "a satanic S. J. Perelman . . . by way of Disney and de Sade." The path my little comic novel followed to a review in the *New York Times* seemed as haphazard and accidental as the manner of its composition. Tom McGuane had recently sold his first novel to Simon and

Schuster and it was hard to stifle my envy when he was cor-
recting his galleys while I stacked boxes of breakfast cereal at
the store. In those days, Tom and I showed each other our
works in progress, offering advice and hopefully helpful critical commentary. When he kept asking to see what I was
working on, I remained evasive. Making the whole thing up
as I went along, page by page, seeking only to amuse myself
in the process, I had no idea at all where my foolish experiment was going. Finally, Tom persuaded me to let him take
the first forty pages home to read over the weekend.

"Quite possibly the finest comic novel ever written in
America." McGuane's candid assessment the following
Monday flabbergasted me. Tom insisted he send the pages on
to his editor at S&S. I thought of every possible reason to
decline his generous offer. The book wasn't finished. Worse,
it was only a first draft typed on cheap second-sheet canary
paper and heavily corrected with Magic Marker strike-outs
and ballpoint pen inserts. None of this mattered to Tom. He
said he'd have it Xeroxed at his expense (twenty-five cents a
page seemed a sum to be reckoned with in those impover-
ished buck-an-hour days) and pay for all the postage. In the
end, I relented. What did it matter? I wasn't an aspiring professional writer anymore. I was just a guy who worked for
minimum wage in a grocery.

Two or three weeks later, a call came for me at Jack Pep-
per's General Store in Bolinas, California. This in itself

wasn't unusual. Too poor at the time to afford the luxury of a telephone, I often gave out the store's number to anyone needing to get hold of me in a hurry. The enthusiastic voice on the other end belonged to Richard Locke from Simon and Schuster. He loved *Alp* and wanted to publish the book. S&S would pay me a $2,000 advance, a thousand bucks on signing and another grand upon their acceptance of a finished manuscript. At the end of my shift, I untied my stock boy's apron and walked out of the store into the rest of my life.

The following year, part of the prepublication publicity for *Alp* involved my inclusion in a *Life* magazine article about "young authors." I didn't feel all that young back then. At twenty-eight, I was the same age as Stephen Crane when he died. Nevertheless, I told the interviewer that I wrote novels "on whim," a bit of an exaggeration as it certainly didn't apply to either of my other two unpublished manuscripts. This was the period of the world's first heart transplant operations and one night, high at a party, I made a wisecrack to the effect that if medical science kept moving in this direction, one day we'd just throw away our vulnerable bodies and simply preserve our brains in some elaborate home entertainment center. Adrift in my hangover the next morning, I thought that if I did actually write novels on whim, I might as well go for a spin with my crazy brain notion. The end result, after a year of work, was *Gray Matters*.

Whereas *Alp* almost seemed to write itself and I flew through a first draft in less than six months, this new as-yet-untitled brain project went a lot slower. At first, under the influence of Samuel Beckett or, perhaps, Dalton Trumbo, I endeavored to write the book in the first person. Wasn't a brain floating in a fish tank the ultimate first person singular? I also decided to use the present tense. Why not describe the future as the present? This time the influence was Joyce Carey's exquisite novel, *Mr. Johnson*. The problem, after thirty pages or so, was that nothing was happening. My little brain just floated in solitude, thinking his random thoughts, while the story remained utterly static.

After my false start in a borrowed New York City apartment, I ventured out to Montana for the first time and started again from scratch in a little cabin at Chico Hot Springs near Yellowstone Park. It was the summer of Woodstock and the first moon landing, aside from the ongoing horrors of Vietnam, a time of hope and promise. I salvaged a few odds and ends out of those unusable first pages. The original nameless brain had evolved into Skeets. I also came up with the concept of memory-merge and had some idea of the mechanized world wherein Skeets dwelled. He had watched the films of a Czech actress named Vera Mitlovic and studied the work of Obu Itubi, an African sculptor, so I arbitrarily made them characters in the book. For structure, I fell back on the quick-cutting character jumps I had used in *Alp* and started making the new draft up day by day as I went along. True to my word, I wrote the novel on whim.

I finished the first draft of *Gray Matters* in Barra de Navidad, Mexico, during the winter of 1970. It was only ninety pages long. Buying into Hemingway's notion that an iceberg achieved its "dignity of motion" because two-thirds of its bulk remained under the surface, I left out about half of my story and sent it off to New York with my fingers crossed. This time, not only did I have no phone but, when the time came to talk with Simon and Schuster, I had to ride the bus all the way up to Guadalajara in order to make the call. Although my new editor liked what she saw and offered a modest advance, she did observe that the book seemed "terribly short."

Enlarging the novel presented no great difficulty. I already knew the iceberg's underwater size and shape. Geographical shifts provided the major delays. I moved first to Key West and then on to Connecticut before the revisions were finally finished that fall. In the meantime, my agent (bless her mercenary heart) sold the abbreviated ninety-page version to *Playboy* for a sum triple my book advance. *Gray Matters* fared far better in the marketplace than did *Alp*. The novel went into a second hardback printing, had a decent paperback sale and appeared in several foreign editions. (Three cheers for the French, who've kept it continuously in print for over three decades.) Later, it won a 1971 Playboy Editorial Award (Best New Fiction Contributor). Gabriel García Márquez came in second. He went on to win the Nobel Prize, so I guess he doesn't hold any grudges.

Of all the accolades and success garnered by *Gray Matters,* what pleased me the most was a fan letter forwarded by my publisher to my old-fashioned combination-dial mailbox at the post office/general store/gas pump in Pray, Montana. It came unsolicited from John Cheever, one of my all-time favorite authors. He had happened upon my little novel and generously wrote to say he "didn't think anyone could go that far out and bring it off." Cheever said I had done just that and offered his "congratulations and best wishes." My hands trembled every time I reread his brief note. I guess I had committed literature after all.

With my *Playboy* money, I moved my small family to a house overlooking the Caribbean at Playa Bonita, Costa Rica. I had expected to dip my toe into the turbulent ocean of science fiction only a single time, but after the success of *Gray Matters,* the fiction editor at *Playboy* asked me to risk the undertow once again. This was more of an enticement than an actual assignment. Lured by the potential of another fat paycheck, I plunged back in, writing the first draft of *Symbiography* between bouts of bodysurfing during the winter of 1971. Alas, when I submitted the piece, *Playboy* rejected it, as did subsequently a dozen other magazines. Even the pulp rags didn't want it. I felt like the drowning captain on a sinking ship.

A year or so later, Dan Gerber (poet, fiction writer, essayist, formula one racer and small press mogul) read the novella in Montana. He offered to publish the piece as the first in a series of short fiction his Sumac Press planned on releasing. There was a modest advance and a beautiful limited edition. "Another short story done up in hardcover," sniffed the *New York Times*. With only a thousand copies in print, we weren't expecting a best seller. Another year went by. *Penthouse* ran a condensed version of *Symbiography*, calling it "The Dreamer." Later, Embassy Pictures optioned the little book and hired me to develop it into a script. The *L. A. Times* named "Nomad" among the ten best unproduced screenplays in Hollywood. Recently, *Symbiography* was optioned again for three more years. It went from rejection and failure to one of my most successful projects. There's a moral in here somewhere.

Both of the other two short pieces in this collection began as magazine assignments. In the early 1970s, *Playboy* had a plan to replace its "Little Annie Fanny" cartoon parody at the back of the magazine with a more robust science fiction feature. Their idea was to pair a different artist and writer in each issue. The editors contacted me and asked if I'd like to work with French cartoonist Philippe Druillet. As I had been a fan of Druillet's graphic novel, *Les 6 Voyages des Lone Sloane*, I immediately said yes. The assignment demanded finding a narrative form to dovetail with Druillet's abstract geometric style and so I deliberately constructed "Home-coming" without either plot or characters. The little story was well received at *Playboy*. Only one problem remained: of the dozen or so writers who had agreed to contribute to the series, I was the only one who actually delivered a finished piece and so the entire notion was abandoned.

"Homecoming" seemed doomed by its abstract nature to that peculiar limbo inhabited by unpublished manuscripts and unproduced screenplays. I thought no one would ever want a story so specifically designed to accompany illustrations that didn't exist. It turned out I was wrong. When the *Cornell Review*, a high-end literary magazine affiliated with the university, started up in the spring of 1977, I was asked to contribute a story to their first issue. After "Conquistador" had been noted for distinction in *The Best American Short Stories of 1978*, editor Baxter Hathaway requested something new. I sent him "Homecoming." It appeared in issue number five, and in his introduction Hathaway wrote, "Can the reader tell whether William Hjortsberg has tongue in cheek or not . . . ?" Sometimes I wonder myself.

"The Clone Who Ran for Congress" owes its life to Patricia Ryan who, in October 1975, was the text department editor at *Sports Illustrated*. Pat rode herd over all the freelancers contributing material to the magazine. I had worked on several oddball sporting articles for her in the past (avalanche control, raft trips, fly-fishing, rodeo schools), and when she wrote to ask if I'd be interested in writing a science fiction piece about the Olympics ("Maybe cloning?"), I jumped at the chance, not often being offered an opportunity to write fiction on assignment.

Other than the Olympics connection (the summer games were coming around again the next year in Montreal), *Sports Illustrated* gave me free rein. I liked Pat's suggestion about clones as it provided a convenient starting point. A first-person narrative seemed to fit the bill and once I came up with the concept of a disgruntled corporate sports "image modifier" I was off and running. The story took much less time to write than a more conventional piece. Pat liked what she saw and ran it in the magazine almost without alteration, although somewhere along the line the title changed to "Goodby, Goodby, Goodby, Mr. Chips." (Knowing I had also written a comic bullfight novel called *Toro! Toro! Toro!*, this prompted a friend to suggest a mock title for the detective novel I then had in progress: "Kiss Me, Kiss Me, Kiss Me, Deadly.") Curiously, *Sports Illustrated* never used the titles supplied by the actual writers of the articles. It had something to do with layout and the art department but I never understood exactly what. In any case, whatever the title, I truly believe "The Clone Who Ran for Congress" was the only work of science fiction ever published in the magazine.

Life is nothing if not a series of accidents. A blind date in college becomes your first wife. Another chance encounter in a doctor's office waiting room leads to divorce and remarriage. An old pal loans a copy of one of your novels as bedtime reading to a visiting friend who just happens to be Ridley Scott's agent and two years later you're in London working on the tenth draft of an original motion picture. Or, more to the point, while researching a biography of the late poet and novelist Richard Brautigan, I phoned Jack Shoemaker who, in the 1960s, co-owned the Unicorn Book Shop near Santa Barbara where his friend Richard read the entire *Trout Fishing in America* shortly before its first publication. In the course of our interview, Jack happened to ask, "Whatever happened to your book, *Symbiography?*" and the eventual result of that query became this collection.

Having a book go out of print is akin to watching a cherished friend die. Seeing it republished is like participating in a resurrection. Unlike Henry James, who rewrote all his novels when they were reissued, I have for the most part left the work in its original form. Other than proofreading for spelling and grammatical errors that slipped through the first time around, I have largely resisted the temptation to edit myself. I did feel troubled by the repeated use of the word "tape" in both *Gray Matters* and *Symbiography*. Magnetic recording tape is almost obsolete today and surely wouldn't be in use five hundred years into the future, so I amended the term to avoid any anachronisms. Also, we all now know how long a round-trip to Jupiter takes and it isn't three hundred years, so I substituted Aldebaran as a destination. Ditto the date of the 1999 Thirty-Minute War, since that moment in time has come and gone without an outbreak of world-wide hostilities. In addition, I included epigraphs for both books, which were omitted way back when. In the case of *Gray Matters*, I felt it was too pretentious. For *Symbiography*, I thought I was just being silly. I no longer feel the same in either instance and the epigraphs have been duly restored.

The future remains an unwritten book, its cryptic pages blank, and no crystal ball wizard, palm reader or Tarot deck manipulator can accurately provide a sneak preview of what's coming in the next chapter. It is precisely this un-known anything-can-happen aspect of the time yet to come that makes the possibilities presented by science fiction such fertile ground for the literary imagination. Writers are forever looking for new ways to retell old stories. The free-dom provided by speculation about the future allows the artist a means of viewing the present through a fresh pair of eyes. Among the several unfinished projects stacked on a shelf awaiting my further attentions is a novel dealing with time travel (hopefully in a manner fresh enough to make that well-worn path worth yet another visit). Whether I'll ever get around to telling this particular tale becomes a science fic-tion story all its own.

SYMBIOGRAPHY

There's no business like show business . . .

—

IRVING BERLIN

PAR SONDAK'S HOUSE was set on automatic. Beyond the garden, concealed sensory-indicators probed the waiting night. All rooms but one were disconnected until morning, windows and doors sealed, air-conditioners silent; deep in the sub-basement, the accumulator and power-distributor idled. Only Sondak's soundproof studio remained active. There, in the padded, ovoid chamber, Par Sondak slept; his swollen, pink body curled, knees drawn almost to his chest, his thumb in his mouth.

Adjoining the egg-shaped studio hummed a unit housing the encephalograph probes, high-density recorders, mode storage banks, duplication and mix-machinery; the tools of the trade. While the Dreamer slept, folded like an embryo, a circuited crown of receptors and transmitters banded his smooth, unwrinkled brow. This equipment captured and pre-served the subtle essence of his art.

The dream was standard Sondak escape adventure: sword-play, a cut rose, distant hoofbeats on a moonlit road, the awesome stillness of the scaffold. Attention to detail made all of Sondak's dreams memorable; his feeling for place and period was unlike any other Dreamer's. Sondak's career was in its eighty-fifth year and over three-hundred of his dreams remained in public circulation.

Far at the bottom of the hill, among the disorder and rot hidden from the Dreamer's machine-tooled house by the opulence of his gardens, a starved mongrel prowled, sniffing the debris left by encamping Nomads. There wan't much, for the Nomads were themselves avid scavengers, and the dog found nothing of interest among the charred garbage and broken glass; even discarded bones had been gnawed to splinters by the eager rats.

The dog continued up the hill, favoring an injured forepaw, ignorant of the warning implied by the orderly cultivation and the watching infra-red eyes ahead. A hidden sensor relayed the intruder's presence back to the house; the computer plotted the exact location; twin antennae revolved on the turreted roof, focusing a disc-mounted sound-intensifier. The dog lifted his head to catch a final scent as the high-frequency beam found its target. In an instant, the animal's blood temperature rose to the boiling-point and, before he could fall, he erupted from within, consumed by a burst of incandescent flame which left his canine imprint briefly hanging in the evening air, a chalky drift of ashes and smoke like shreds of fog dissolving.

In the morning it was raining. The kitchen switched on at six. Within the hour, the rest of the house came alive and by the time Par Sondak was eased awake electronically, the place was purring like a spaceship.

Smoothly, the sides of the studio slid open and Sondak stepped down, padding across the thermal-turf mat which covered his bedroom floor like a carpet of insulated moss. The mirrored walls reflected the lurching sag of his fatman's amble; sounds of breaking waves issued from a dozen surrounding speakers. Although his house was located a thousand miles from any sea, Sondak found the rushing murmur of surf soothing in the early morning.

The bath was contoured to the folds of his massive body and while churning, scented water swirled and sensitive vibrators kneaded his mottled flesh, the extended nozzle of an air-compression inoculator blasted painlessly through the tallow of his suet-soft buttock, giving him the minimum-daily-requirement; the complete prescription of vitamins, enzymes, hormones and energizers which kept him plodding through another day.

Par Sondak was one-hundred-and-five years old and in the best of health. Indeed, he had never been sick a day of his life. His outward appearance was that of a chubby, middle-aged infant, due mainly to his total baldness, a condition resulting from nearly a century of wearing the probes to bed each night. "Bald as a Dreamer," was the standard cliché.

Par Sondak punched the code-numbers for breakfast and waited.

"Good morning, sir," his computer said. "Did you sleep well?"

"I hope so." Sondak yawned. "What's the weather been like?"

"There was thunderstorm-level precipitation for two hours earlier this morning, and another light shower is scheduled for sixteen."

"How long?"

"The gardeners have requested forty-five minutes."

"No, I want rain all afternoon, clearing at sunset."

"Very good." The computer paused. "Sunset will be at 19:49."

"It doesn't matter, I'll be around. Anything special for today?"

"You have a conference with the City at ten. Otherwise, the agenda is open."

A tray appeared on the conveyor from the kitchen and Sondak carried his breakfast onto the patio, where he sat in the shade of a flowering dogwood. The eggs on his plate were real; Sondak despised synthetics and maintained a poultry yard in his garden. From below came the sounds of the mechanical cultivators at work, weeding and fertilizing. A row of fruit trees screened their synchronized labor. Beyond the gardens stretched the open desert, barren and scorched;

hills like slag-heaps, shining, metallic, sparsely fringed with a feeble growth of scrub. The Dreamer gazed out over his breakfast at this wasteland, to a point in the distant, hard-blue sky, where three fly-speck vultures turned in a drifting spiral.

Beneath the circling carrion-eaters, on a bleak basalt outcrop jutting over a dry riverbed, a Nomad burial platform rested in the gnarled and naked limbs of a long-dead jack pine. Most of the clan departed before sunup, but several Nomads, blood-kin to the child lashed in the branches above them, stood silently waiting for the vultures to feed.

The ritual was complete; offerings had been made and the proper spells cast. But the behavior of the birds was important and the old ones watched for sign, measuring their vatic powers against those of the augur, an ancient crone who hunched and mumbled, fingering an amulet from long ago. The vultures settled in the branches around the body, making a show of folding their wings and shifting from foot to foot while they sized up the gathering below. No one moved. Only the wind, rustling the tinder-dry thornbushes, disturbed the quiet. The largest of the lizard-necked birds hopped forward onto the platform, rasping with a satisfied croak, and thrust his beak into an eye-socket. A good omen: a mutter of approval ran through the grouped Nomads.

One member of the clan wasn't watching: a young man

with only a faint mustache and the first downy patches of beard on his cheeks. He stood apart from the others, gripping the long wire-bound barrel of his smooth-bore muzzle-loader, and stared back across the desolate blast-furnace expanse of cinder-pile nothingness to the glowing green oasis, a brief flowering of life in a dead land. It was the first time the young man had ever seen the fabled, forbidden dwelling-place of a Lord Citizen, the Select and All-Powerful Ones.

Of all the rooms in his efficient house, the projection-booth was one Sondak almost never used. He disliked the cramped, windowless chamber; the dull uniformity of its metallic walls, ceiling and floor. Seated in the padded control seat in the center of this tiny room, Sondak felt uncomfortably claustrophobic and he avoided coming here except when called in by conferences.

Sondak wasn't alone for long. A door appeared to open in the blank, gray wall and the hologram image of a Dream Syndicate hostess stepped into the room. The girl was young and not unattractively dressed in a plum-colored tunic, her nipples tinted pale green to match her lips and hair.

"Prompt as always," Sondak said.

"That's how things happen in the City." The girl smiled. "Promptly. What setting would you like for the conference, sir?"

"Makes no difference to me. Anything but this iron maiden."

The girl turned for a moment and nodded to the wall behind her. "Well, if it's all right with you, sir," she said, "Mr. Tarquille is already adjusted to setting number ZT-90065-N7."

Sondak slowly repeated the number under his breath, tapping it out on the keypad set into the arm of the control seat. The walls shimmered, an instant silver rainfall as the strict confines of the projection-booth gave way to distant, snow-bright mountains and Sondak found himself and his padded chair on the bank of a crystalline lake, facing Omar Tarquille under the scented boughs of a wind-stirred spruce.

"Morning, Par," the Executive said, intent on the legs of the hostess as she wandered off among the pines. "You're looking fit."

"How can you tell?" Sondak laughed to see Tarquille's momentary, throat-clearing discomfort. "Still fond of alpine scenery, I see, Omar."

"A placid setting is best for conferences, don't you think?"

"Oh, I'm not so sure. Perhaps more would be accomplished in crisis; on the deck of a sinking ship, let's say."

The Executive chuckled pleasantly. "Been dreaming lately, Par?"

"Every night for a month."

"Glad to hear it. Must feel good to be back in action. How long will this one run, do you think?"

"Final mix is still a long way off, but I'd estimate at least ten hours."

"Perfect, Par, absolutely perfect. You've got a lot of fans here in the City waiting for a new one, you know."

"That's reassuring to hear."

"The name Sondak still draws an audience, never mind statistics telling you Direct-Experience-Modes outsell Dreams four-to-one in the preference-ballots."

"Figures are meaningless to me, Omar." The Dreamer yawned behind the back of his hand.

"How old are you now, Par, anyway? Over two-hundred?"

"No, just a hundred-and-five."

"Ah, still a young man." The Executive fingered his chin and raised an eyebrow, in imitation of the sage he thought himself to be. "Much too young to be off hiding in the wilderness like a hermit. You belong here in the City, where decisions are made. Do you good to be among men, keeping up with the times. When you get to be a four-century-old fart like me, why then you can hole up in a crypt out in the middle of nowhere."

"I like it here out in the middle of nowhere." The Dreamer stared across at the image of a lake where rising trout disrupted the reflected mountains.

"It would be different if you had some company, Par.

Someone young and athletic, like that little hostess in here a minute ago; or a boy, depending on . . . preferences. But to be alone is unnatural, and if you don't mind an old-timer like me butting in, I'll say that too much solitude is bad for your work."

Sondak did mind an old-timer butting in. He liked being alone, and said so.

"Surrounded by Nomad savages, how can you stand it?"

"I was watching a group of Nomads this morning at breakfast. First I've seen in over a year."

The Executive nodded politely and changed the subject, saying he was anxious to spend a night soon with Sondak's new dream.

"I'll put a mode on the waves as soon as final mix is in."

"Very good. Can I get you anything from the City? Landermann has a new Dream, a regular nightmare, I'm told."

"No thanks. I've too much work."

"All right. If something comes up I'll arrange a conference." Omar Tarquille smiled, gave a slight wave, and vanished from the lakefront. In the distance, a quail called sharply.

The Dreamer punched the off button. The mountains melted and shrank like a reflection on water seeping into sand. Par Sondak was back in his projection-booth. He pushed his bulk out of the chair and started for the door, eager for fresh air. Although the booth was a favored plaything with City-dwellers, where space was at a premium and the only open country was on mode, Sondak preferred sitting on his patio or roaming in the garden to any of his vast file of electronic voyages. The computer still scheduled theatrical events in the booth each week, but Sondak seldom went. Conferences were all he used his booth for these days.

The Dreamer was smiling as he stepped onto the patio. "Imagine Omar offering up Landermann's new dream." Sondak never played the dreams of others. He had no interest in them. His dream-table was a piece of equipment he used even less often than the projection-booth. Dreams were not his kind of diversion.

Buick of the Cincinnati clan crouched in the shade of the dead tree, watching. A warrior since the age of twelve, when his father was killed in a skirmish with the Lafayette County people and care of the family gun passed to him as eldest male, Buick wore the name-brands of six slain enemies sewn on leather thongs to his belt. No spoils were taken from his father's body; his own people had the victory that day, and the grief-stricken boy hammered the ancient brass emblem into the carved stock of the family gun, continuing his mourning fast well beyond the ceremonial three days after the dead man's charm-bag was secretly buried. Buick believed this token brought him luck; more luck than any of the talismans in the snakeskin pouch hanging from his belt; he fingered his father's name-brand: JEEP, worn smooth and shiny from constant rubbing.

The young Nomad was in need of luck today. All his childhood long, he listened to cooking-fire tales of the magic places where men lived like Gods. At the clan chants, he thrilled to the epic songs of Texaco, the Firechief, mounted on his flying horse, how he stole the light-that-never-dies from the citadel of the Lord Citizens. Until this morning, only a handful of the Elders had ever seen the enchanted gardens, their recollections, hoarded like treasure from the past. And yet, these same boastful old men squawked now of the All-Powerful One's wrath and demanded a girl-child be sacrificed to protect their long, white beards. Let them all scamper bowlegged into the brush, Buick of Cincinnati was a warrior and carried the family gun; he was battle-tested and would admit to fearing no man, not even the favorites of the Gods. From the moment he first saw the serene silver towers rising out of the unbelievable green of the surrounding oasis, he knew that he could not rest until he walked in the shade of those magic trees and plucked the fruit from their forbidden limbs.

One room in Par Sondak's mechanical house was unlike the others. The walls here were panelled in walnut, with carved Ionic pilasters and egg-and-dart molding. There was a real fireplace framing brass andirons and birch logs. In place of extruded plastic furniture were wingchairs upholstered in dark green leather and on the floor, the swirling blue lotus buds of a hand-knotted Kirman. Above the mantel hung the Velazquez portrait of Pope Innocent X. It was a stately, secluded room; silent as a meditation garden; a sanctuary. With the exception of the unused Public Reading Room at the City-Center, it was the largest library left on Earth.

Par Sondak sat in an armchair by one of the tall leaded-glass windows, a calf-bound volume of Gibbon's superb history open on his knees. Around him, in alcoves along the walls, were shelves ranked with books, rising to the ceiling in rich strata of red, green and maroon morocco. The Dreamer gazed out the window at the sculpted hedges delineating his gardens, unable to read. An irritation remained from this morning's conference: the tone in Omar Tarquille's voice when he mentioned the popularity of Direct-Experience-Modes. Sondak wondered how much of a threat was intended by the crafty Executive.

Ten years before, the complexities of the encephalograph probes and neural receptors were miniaturized to a near-microscopic wafer, and Sondak had known there would be no shortage of rogues and daredevils volunteering for surgical implantation; but what he never guessed at the time was the size of the audience that would be attracted to participating in hand-to-hand gladiatorial combat or one-man rocket races to the moon and back. D.E.M.s of assassination and torture were even available. Every space drifter and mercenary killer in the City wore a mini-probe under his scalp, ready to double the take from a hazardous assignment by selling the modes to the highest bidder.

Suicide and murder remained the two highest contributors to the deathrate in the City, with accidents a paltry third and disease only a memory. A near-eternal life-span froze the eminent in a static hierarchy, like prehistoric mammoths preserved in a glacier's epochal crawl. Par Sondak was a very rich man. In the City he would be an easy target for the ambitious. The Dreamer's gentle, retiring nature was a distinct liability in a society which encouraged ruthlessness and cunning. Sondak knew whenever his dreams failed to score appreciably on the preference-ballot (and the inevitable day was coming when large-cast D.E.M.s would be as extravagantly staged as any hologram spectacular), his credit-rating would no longer support his isolated and independent life and he would be forced to give up the peace of his library for the sophisticated power-struggle within the stately corridors of the City.

The young Nomad paused at the bottom of the hill to check the primer in the frizzen-pan of his musket and wind the wheel lock back until the action was cocked. He concealed his bed-roll and saddlebags between two large stones and took only what he would carry into battle: shot and powder, a goat-skin waterbag, his bone-hilted cutlass and the protective magic of his charm-bag. His hair was tied back in a warrior's top-knot. His name-brand hung around his neck on a braided cord, flashing in the sun; a challenge to anything he might encounter.

Buick stepped forward into the rain, stooping as if he were entering a tent. Outside, the empty desert burned under a raging sun, but beyond the gentle enclosing waterfall stands of elm and oak and maple billowed like deciduous cumuli. Buick removed the homespun shirt, his sacred number, 66, patched on front and back, and wrapped it around the lock of his musket, held muzzle downward against the fine, mist-like rain. He felt drunk and giddy with so much unfamiliar greenness.

At the edge of the woods were fruit orchards and a snarl of blackberry brambles in the open clearing. The Nomad crouched behind a tree trunk, smelling the sweetness of windfalls fermenting in the wet grass. With the musket cradled in his arms, Buick rolled onto his stomach, head low as he began to crawl. Through the even rows of trees, beyond the surrounding gardens, he saw the turreted rooftop where a disk-mounted sound-intensifier began to pivot.

In the library, a tall Hepplewhite pendulum clock with hanging brass weights and the phases of the moon in a hand-painted procession around the age-stained pasteboard face chimed the hour. Par Sondak closed the volume of Gibbon; at the sideboard, he filled a tulip-shaped glass with blackberry brandy distilled from fruit he had picked himself. He remembered the thorn scratches on his soft white hands with considerable pride. What would they say in the City about such hands, berry-stained and bleeding, hands that had done work?

As a rule, the Dreamer wandered naked in the house, adding only a conical hat to protect his tender scalp from the sun in the gardens; but, for the library, he wore a long, shot-silk gown, cut in the flowing style of a medieval cassock. The current fashion for men in the City, ballooning knee-britches and short metal-scaled vests, struck Sondak as ridiculous, like the costumes trained bears wore in the ancient circuses. He thought of the portly Gibbon, unable to rise from his knees after proposing marriage; could his own age boast such a droll genius? Was there someone to record the decline and fall of the Utopian Era?

The computer interrupted the Dreamer's musing. "Excuse me, sir," the modulated, unhurried voice never varied; the computer announced good news and bad alike with the same laconic indifference. "The sensors report the presence of an intruder on the grounds. A Nomad, sir."

"Where is he now?"

"The last fix placed him on the edge of the south orchard."

"Have the arrangements all been made?"

"Everything according to your specifications."

"Good." The Dreamer finished his brandy in a single swallow. "Very good. It's only a matter of time and he's ours. See if you can pick him up on holo; I want to watch from the control room." Sondak's face was flushed. He left the library, lifting the skirt of his long gown above his ankles like an anxious priest as he hurried up the gleaming corridor.

Buick kneeled beside the base of one of a dozen fluted marble columns surrounding an ornamental pond. Only a broad swath of immaculate green lawn separated his hiding-place from the curving crystal and silver minarets of the house. He never planned on coming this far. Simply to have stolen some fruit would have been sufficient triumph; to risk this much was madness. But Buick was following a scent which lured him still, past any thought of danger. He was intoxicated by the wind-borne aroma of roasting meat. Now he was close enough to hear the sizzle of melting fat and see pennants of white smoke reaching through the rain from below the circular terrace.

Buick covered the distance to the stairs in five long strides, nearly slipping on the wet flagstones before he reached the shelter of a carved balustrade. He started down, one step at a time, his back pressed against the rough ashlar masonry of the terrace wall. At the bottom, out of sight of the house, stood a hidden pavilion and under the blue and gold awnings, a spitted calf turned, glazed and dripping, over a bed of coals.

Of all the wonders seen today, the splendor of food in such profusion was by far the most magical and bewitching. The Nomad wandered spellbound in front of a long cloth-covered table, trying to associate trout jellied in aspic, terrine of pheasant, grilled spring lamb, fruit heaped on silver platters with his own memories of eating roots and porridge, when a bit of dog or an occasional rat trapped among the grainsacks was a prize addition to the stewpot.

The rain whispered against the taut canopy of the pavilion; the coals hissed and snapped. Buick waited, barely moving. There wasn't much time. The banquet table was prepared, the guests must not be far behind. Although his every instinct told him to hurry, Buick approached the feast with the dignity of an invited God.

A hind-quarter from the broiled calf stood on a thick wooden salver. The Nomad leaned his musket against the table and cut a slice with a surgically keen carving-knife. He had never tasted anything so good. He would take as much meat as he could carry. The knife, too. It was a beautiful knife; no one else in the clan owned such a knife. He leaned forward and cut another slice.

"Good, good," the voice behind him said. "Eat."

The Nomad spun about, grabbing for his musket, gagging

on a mouthful of meat. His instincts had betrayed him. He wasn't alone. A pink-faced, hairless fat man stood only feet away, his long silk robe shining in the fire-light. "Don't be alarmed," the Lord Citizen said. "Eat what you want. Take. This is for you."

Buick steadied his musket against his shoulder and fired. The Lord's face was lost for a moment in the sulfurous smoke, but his smile was intact when the air cleared. Buick knew this was magic. His gun carried a load of scrap-metal; ancient bottlecaps, nails, screws and bolts; rusted, unrecognizable lumps from the machine age found anywhere in the desert by scratching the surface with a stick. In battle, warriors reloaded by scooping handfuls of the stuff off the ground. With a three-ounce charge of crude black powder behind it, the load erupted from the smooth-bore like a swarm of angry bees. At close range, there was no such thing as missing. Buick was fighting a phantom. He drew his cutlass and rushed forward, wildly carving the empty air.

"Do you see? Do you see?" Par Sondak exulted among the displays and monitors of the control room. The image of the Nomad slashing with his sword appeared on rows of holo screens arranged along the far wall: close-ups, wide-angles from above, teleholo views. "Look at him. Isn't he a savage?" The Dreamer switched off the hologram-projector and addressed the bewildered face on the three-dimensional wall displays. "It is useless to fight. You cannot harm me. You are at the mercy of my power." Sondak turned off the audio. "How much longer before it takes effect?"

"Within three to five minutes, sir," the computer said. "If the dosage were any higher it would kill him."

"I'll keep him amused." The Dreamer switched the hologram back on and turned up the volume. The Nomad was gasping and bug-eyed when the fat man in the shining robe reappeared on the other side of the table. "Why be my enemy?" smiled the cherubic pink Lord, extending his open palms in a gesture of friendship. "This food is for you."

Buick stared, fear-struck and open-mouthed.

"Can't you speak?" the Dreamer asked. "What's your name?"

On the bank of displays, a dozen mouths soundlessly formed a single word.

"Well, you do understand something, don't you? Speak a little louder. I'm not going to hurt you."

The Nomad's hand groped for his face and throat. His mouth opened and closed, fighting for air like a stranded fish. Teeth bared in a snarl of final defiance, he hurled his cutlass at the smiling figure of the Lord and pitched headlong onto the elegant table, dragging a torrent of silver and crystal after him in his fall to the floor. Par Sondak's smile remained unchanged. He gave some orders and switched off the hologram.

Fresh from the laundry, sanitized and fumigated, the Nomad's garments and weapons were displayed on a table in the main hall of the Dreamer's house. Par Sondak examined each item with care. He fingered the unfamiliar roughness of hand-woven fabric and toyed with the primitive spring-wound ratchets in the firing mechanism of the heavy wheel lock musket. In a sudden moment of boyish enthusiasm, he shouldered the awkward weapon, pressing his cheek against the brass-studded stock.

The Nomad's belongings facinated the Dreamer. He was puzzled by the red numerals sewn to the coarse shirt, but he recognized the metal-and-ceramic medallions hanging on the leather belt as products of the Late Industrial Age. One showed a clipper ship under full sail; others portrayed faces: the head of an Indian, a bearded Spanish *conquistador*, the Roman god, Mercury, with his winged, soup-bowl helmet; the simplest, a plain white oval, had the word *Ford* across the center in the fluid strokes of the ancient script.

The contents of the snakeskin pouch were equally mysterious. Aside from a few steel ball-bearings and a magnet, the Dreamer could identify none of the other relics and he asked the computer to run a source check with the micro-mode archive in the City. In less than a minute, the picture-wall switched on and a photo-collage appeared; an instant mural display of the objects spilled across the glass table.

"These items," said the computer, "are products of the Late Industrial Age, more than a century before the founding of the Utopian Era. Most of them are machine parts and the pictures are from manufacturer's catalogues which survive from that period. The first, shown on the far left, was a device known as a 'spark plug,' which provided the ignition in the fossil-fuel, internal-combustion engines of a wheeled ground vehicle called an 'automobile.'"

"Cars," Par Sondak said, turning the sparkplug over in his hand.

"What was that, sir?"

"In the vernacular they were called 'cars.'"

"I didn't know you had an interest in that Age, sir."

"Oh, I've read the literature."

"Would you be interested in seeing some film on the subject? The archives have a number of old advertisements preserved. They're only two-dimensional, but they provide an approximation of how these vehicles . . . these 'cars,' must have looked in operation on the ancient highways."

"Go ahead," said Sondak, settling into a contour-chair.

The picture-wall blinked and the photo-mural was replaced by a view down an empty two-lane road, a band of asphalt slicing the verdant landscape. A red-and-white automobile, bright with chromium trim, speeds smoothly through the rushing green.

> See the U.S.A.,
> In your Chevrolet,
> America keeps asking you to call. . . .

For the first time in months, Par Sondak missed the sunset. No one bothered to program new instructions for the kitchen and supper was served as usual on the patio, where it sat and grew cold until the serving-cart rolled out at dusk to clear the table and chase away the gathered song birds. The Dreamer spent the entire afternoon and well into the night watching antique television commercials from the Late Industrial Age. He learned that Mercury and Ford and Buick were the names given to cars by the romantic mercenaries of that time. Imagine, names for machines! The relics from the snakeskin pouch were likewise identified: along with ball-bearings and spark plugs, the Nomad included among his treasures a vacuum tube, three automotive fuses, a flashlight bulb and a tiny six-pointed metal star which had once been used by children in a ball-game known as "jacks."

The Dreamer stared through the glass partition at the unconscious form stretched on his back for diagnosis in the automated clinic. Sondak only half-listened to the medical report. The computer told him that his "guest" was free from any contagious diseases and suffered only from malnutrition and the annoyance of four different species of body-vermin. Although full-grown, the Nomad stood no taller than the average ten-year-old City child and weighed even less; a frail body, marked with savage scars which froze the battle-agony of his wounds forever into his flesh.

"How old is he?" Sondak asked.

The computer's answer comes instantaneously: "Bone tissue analysis indicates no more than fifteen or sixteen years."

"So young . . ." The Dreamer contemplated the lean, weathered features of his captive, who appeared to have experienced more in a few short years than he had in over a century of living. Sondak frowned, troubled by the implications of this momentary self-awareness. He saw, as if for the first time, the strict limits of his cloistered life. He felt imprisoned by a wall of books. The pleasures he took: berry-picking, puttering in the garden, surprising rabbits and deer while walking in the woods, eating organic foods, watching the sunset, all seemed tame when confronted by the scar-striped body of the young Nomad. Par Sondak's adventuring took place in the shadowy realm of dreams; how pale his most stirring Renaissance fantasy appeared when he compared the cloak-and-dagger posturing of his wicked Cardinals and *condottiere* with even one day of life among the nomadic desert tribes.

In the end, Sondak's scholarly nature overcame his dissatisfaction. For hundreds of years, the City's enlightened citizenry had ignored the Nomads exiled outside her air-conditioned walls. More was known about the lichens growing on Mars than about this forgotten portion of mankind. Any research was in the tradition of Mendel and Darwin and Czolwirtzki. The quest for knowledge was itself a great adventure.

The Dreamer's house possessed equipment which would allow him to sample the Nomad's dreams if he desired. Not one secret of this savage subconscious need elude him. But Sondak had more ambitious intentions. Before leaving the automated clinic, he gave the computer orders to begin preparations for surgery. The operation was a simple one. Cerebral mini-probe implantation could be accomplished in less than half-an-hour.

The Dreamer waited in his library. He stood, gazing into the fire, letting his thoughts ride on the snake's-tongue flicker of the flames like a boat adrift on a shifting sea. The computer would announce when everything was ready. Even now, the Nomad youth was being transported to the north, hundreds of kilometers from Sondak's house. In the clinic, the boy had been immunized against every known disease, his teeth treated for decay, his blood refortified and his enzymes renewed. A thorough overhaul ensured that each of his parts would operate as efficiently as the wafer-thin neural-probe wired into his frontal lobe.

Along with the gift of restored health, Sondak added a few useful tools: the tungsten-bladed carving knife which never needed sharpening; a pocket solar-torch, rechargeable even on cloudy days; an assortment of concentrated vitamins, energizers and cellular nutrients, enough to sustain the Nomad's strength no matter how insufficient his diet; and a carefully programmed dream explaining how he came to possess these marvels, a narrative designed to satisfy the boy's heroic expectations as well as his curiosity.

The experiment was working nicely. Soon, the Nomad would be back on his own in a world as alien to the Dreamer's mechanical civilization as the colonies of protoplasmic bubbles floating in the ammonia-clouds obscuring the face of Jupiter. Wherever the Nomad went, whatever strange adventures he encountered, Par Sondak would be there too, exploring the unknown while sealed in the padded security of his egg-shaped studio.

Buick opened his eyes. He lay at the edge of a water hole, across from where a chestnut stallion, hobbled front-leg-to-back, bent to touch noses with his reflection. The boy smiled, watching the horse drink. It was real after all. He hadn't dreamed those weeks alone, or his adventures in the palace of the Lord Citizen. It had all really happened.

Busy with the morning's camp chores, Buick had ample occasion to relive his triumph in memory: he started his cooking fire with the light-that-never-dies and cut slabs of smoked meat with his fine new knife. Behind him, he heard the horse whisking away flies. He was not the same as other men. He had been tested and proved worthy by the All-Powerful.

Until a month ago, a swaybacked donkey stolen during a raid on an encampment of the Buford Creek people was the finest mount Buick ever owned. Now, he rode a stallion bred by the hand of a Lord. The young Nomad remembered the final warning of his host: when you ride away from here, never return; forever shun the dwelling places of the Lord Citizens. It was strange how he understood every word even though the language the Select One spoke was completely unfamiliar to him. Wasn't this another sign?

Buick knew that life was forever changed; his fate altered the moment he stepped through the rain into the world of myth. What other warrior had ever battled a pack of three-headed dogs or been carried across a lake of fire in the talons of a giant hawk? And the victory feast in the rainbow palace of the Lord, how many clansmen could boast such an honor? The ordeal had been an initiation; the feast, with its attendant marvels and magic gifts, a celebration of his success. His was a special destiny.

That night, Par Sondak violated the most cherished of his professional ethics: he interrupted the course of a Dream before visualization was complete. Often it took months while his shifting mental tides brought to the surface sufficient subconscious debris, the odd and often unrelated details which eventually would blend into a cohesive and continuous narrative. The Dreamer understood the evanescent nature of his art. If he missed a night before enough material accumulated for mixing, he ran the risk of having his fantasy unravel before it was successfully off the loom.

It was a chance he was willing to take. The prospect of tuning in the implanted transmitter's signal was too enticing for Sondak and when he placed the receptors on his head and stepped into the studio he issued new instructions for the computer. These were quite complex; he was planning a journey of over a month and needed to program a regimen of daily intravenous feeding and enzyme inoculation. The dream-table would have been more convenient, as it was portable and could have been moved alongside the clinic, but it was also designed to allow for easy interruption; the probe-receptors were set into a cushioned head-rest and merely the sound of a voice in the room or the melodic tone of a confer-ence call-signal was enough to wake a dreamer. The studio was soundproof and temperature controlled. It sealed with the precision of an air lock. Par Sondak left orders that he was not to be disturbed.

Buick reined in at the top of the hill to wait. Across the open plain, he could see the rising dust of six horsemen. He had seen them first shortly after dawn and they followed his trail all morning, coming gradually closer. Buick dismounted, unloading his horse in the shade of a large boulder. He was in no hurry; let them ride their mounts to death in the noon sun. He had known from the start he would have to make a stand; it was a matter of picking the right spot.

Behind the cover of the boulders, Buick primed and cocked his musket, setting it aside where it was easily reached. He unsheathed his cutlass and slipped the blade under his braided belt. If it came to shot and steel he wanted to be ready. The horsemen were at the bottom of the hill, within five-hundred paces. They formed a line, six-abreast, and started up the slope, picking their way through the thorns.

Buick waited until the six were within a hundred paces, but still safely out of musket-range, before he stepped into view. The riders came to a halt at the unexpected sight of an unarmed opponent. One of them pointed to the shining silver box in his hands and laughed when the boy called out his warrior's greeting: *"Ya Buick; m'papa Jeep, fum Cin'natti. Plus-plus breed mi altime conga so!"*

"Waya, chico!" the one who pointed shouted back derisively. It was an insult not to declare your name and lineage.

Buick made a few final adjustments. He learned the fearsome capabilities of the light-that-never-dies the first morning after leaving the palace of the Lord Citizen. The sounds of six wheel locks being wound and the impatient hoof-clatter of the horses carried up the long hillside. *"Okay, chico,"* the men laughed, starting to advance.

Buick focused his instrument and pushed a button. A beam, bright and lightning-quick, oscillated through the still noontime and incinerated the first rider in an instant. Thorn bushes and cactus ignited. A wall of fire swept across the hillside. The horses reared back, plunging and kicking. One lost its footing and went over on top of the rider, a full-bearded ruffian who was impaled on the broken shaft of the lance slung across his shoulder. The others stampeded back down the hill, manes and tails aflame, the men slapping at their burning clothes as they fought for balance.

"*Buick di Cin'natti,*" the boy screamed after them. "*Farchiff! Chi'uillas car un'men al: ya farchiff.*"

In the air-conditioned studio, Par Sondak watched the horsemen retreating like run-away comets. The hot sun made him squint as he climbed off the boulder. In almost every way, he was Buick of Cincinatti: the boy's perceptions were his reality; he felt the exhilarated heartbeat calming; the exultant, victorious cries came from his own throat. And yet, at the same time, he knew that the magic instrument in his hand was an ordinary solar-torch, and while the boy walked down the scorched and smoking hillside and collected the name-brands from the charred remains of his enemies, Par Sondak lay comfortably on his left side, sucking his thumb.

Next morning, in the first silver light of the false dawn, Buick rode to the top of the ridge and surveyed the coming miles from behind a pile of rimrock. On the plain below, colorful circular tents stretched by the hundreds into a haze of ground fog and wood smoke. He counted the banners of a dozen different clans. Never before had he seen so many horses. Buick decided to wait for nightfall, but no skulking through the bushes like a beaten dog. He would ride straight into the heart of the encampment with the light-that-never-dies bright as the newly risen sun in his arms. He envisioned the entire awestruck tribe kneeling before him; even the elders would touch their foreheads to the ground in homage. No other warrior was protected by magic as potent as his.

The hillside was striated with late afternoon shadows as Buick watched a solitary rider following his track through the shrub. The man appeared to be unarmed but Buick was taking no chances and the light-that-never-dies was ready in his hand when he stepped from out of his hiding-place. Before he could utter a word, the stranger made a gesture of peace and greeted him by name: *"Salud, Buick. Mi capo, el Kodak, say'm sooperhowdi yo. Ya Esso de Cleeflan."*

A Clevelander! Buick calmed an urge to burn him from the saddle, but the instinctive hatred showed clearly on his face.

"Mira." The man called Esso reached beneath the folds of his cloak. Buick's finger poised over the button on the side of the silver box but the stranger was holding only an innocuous brown-leather case. *"Fum mi capo, el Kodak,"* he said, handing it down to the boy. *"Gib'm vos yo, farchiff. Summa nostra plusplus volcan. Kodak altime amichee w'Buick."*

Buick ran his hand over the smooth texture of the snap-fastened case. It wasn't made of leather. It was much better than that. It was plastic; stitched by machine. He opened the cover and slid the perfectly preserved mechanism into view. (Par Sondak recognized the instrument as an ancient pair of binoculars.) *"Speks,"* the boy whispered reverently. Several in his clan owned burning-glasses, and once an Elder explained how in olden days men wore these things in their eyes and could see for miles. Buick looked the wrong way through the lenses and very nearly dropped the priceless object in astonishment. *"Ma'nifico,"* he managed to stammer at last.

While the Clevelander unsaddled his horse, Buick went to bring the waterbag. It was his duty to extend hospitality to this stranger, but he vowed not to make the mistake of falling asleep. He would remain on his guard until morning. He wasn't fooled by the fancy gift. The bigger the trap, the better the bait.

Together, they travelled through the night, Buick following Esso's lead from a safe and watchful distance. There was no moon, and the starlit sky arched over the dark landscape like the frozen surface of an inverted lake. They avoided the encampment beyond the ridge. These were renegades, Esso explained; Kodak's enemies. Spies in their camp brought the story of Buick and his magic powers.

Sunrise revealed a sloping valley, rimmed by jagged lime-stone cliffs. Down the center wandered the broad avenue of a dry river-bed, cobbled with bleached water-strewn boulders. The trail led up along the bank and soon they reached a series of small pools, the water cupped and still under the fierce cloudless sky. While the horses drank, and before fill-ing the waterbags, they shared a bit of hard bread and a few strands of sun-dried goat meat.

Further along, the random pools were fed by a feeble flow that seeped and trickled among the stones. Patches of deter-mined grass grew in the streambed and the banks were shaded by willows and cottonwoods. Around noontime, they came to the first of the irrigation dams. Above the dam, the river was full and deep. Buick was amazed at the interconnected canals and ditches dividing the patchwork of green ploughed fields that patterned the valley almost to the distant hills. Except for the gardens of the Lord Citizen, the boy had seen nothing in his short life to equal this extensive cultivation.

The path they followed widened into a regular highway, furrowed with cart-tracks and scored by the hoof-prints of innumerable horses. Side-roads paralleled the irrigation canals into the fields and at regular intervals tall stone watchtowers stood guard over the workers who paused and waved to the passing riders. Once, they had to wait near the side of the road while a troop of thirty or more armed horse-men went by at a trot. These men wore no numbers on their shirts; instead, the hinged plates of their leather and brass armor were partly concealed by flapping white tabards, all identically marked with the sign of the cross.

It was late afternoon when they passed through the main gate into the village. The headless bodies of three Nomads hung by their heels from the crossbeam. The heads, along with a dozen others, bloated sun-blackened crow-bait, stood impaled on sharpened stakes that bristled like spines on a lizard's back along the sinuous mud wall surrounding the village.

To Buick, who had spent most of his life in tents, the low angular flat-roofed buildings seemed dark and uninviting. Like the wall, they were built of dried mud and stones. In every doorway, small naked children stood, watching them pass. Occasionally, one of the bolder ones risked a somber smile.

In the center of the village rose the steep stone ramparts of the Grand Dragon's fortress, where numbers of squat ugly houses pressed together against the great wall like piglets squirming among the protective teats of a sleeping sow. The arched entranceway, built high above the ground, could be reached only by a narrow wooden chute, designed to be winched safely up and into place in time of siege. As they rode single-file up this gangplank, Buick observed the snub muzzles of several bronze cannon protruding from between the saw-toothed crenelations above. And from the highest tower streamed the long, white, fork-tailed banner of the Orthodoxy, the blood-red cross furling and undulant in the wind.

In the open courtyard, grooms hurried to stable their horses. Esso departed with a formal bow, leaving Buick in the hands of three fawning servants, who led the way inside, carrying his saddlebags and musket. They brought him through vaulted corridors and winding stairs to a suite of well-lit, high-ceilinged rooms. The arched windows commanded a view of the entire valley. The floors were tiled and covered with bold carpets, woven in the traditional pattern of red-and-white stripes and five-pointed stars. Sacred relics were set in niches along the walls. (Far away, the Dreamer identified the radiator grill and steering-wheel of an automobile, a coin-operated telephone, and the pearly-pink ovals of four plastic toilet-seats.) In the center of the room stood a large, battered, red-metal box with the word *oca-Col* embossed on the dented facade. (This remained a mystery even to the somnolent Sondak.)

In one room, a sunken bath steamed; in another, a festive meal waited on a low table; a third, with its hanging canopies and cushion-covered mats, held the promise of much-needed sleep. Buick was ushered through each of these chambers by the obsequious trio and finally, bathed, massaged and fed, he was left alone with a slim dark-eyed girl who slipped out of her simple gown and stepped under the tent-like canopy, where she introduced the wild Nomad boy (and the enthusiastic Sondak), to pleasures more refined than those he was accustommed to grapple for on the cold night-time desert sand.

The white robe hung several sizes too large, but the length corrected by adjusting the sash and the ample sleeves nicely concealed the silver shape of the light-that-never-dies, dangling from Buick's wrist by a leather thong. His companion, Xerox, wore the hoodless, blue-and-gold robe of a Knight in the Order. They walked side-by-side without talking, down passageways bright with morning sunshine. At the far end of a courtyard enclosed by overhanging galleries, a gate was opened by two sentries. Above their heads, the mysterious wrought iron characters, B&O R.R., bloomed among the filigree.

Inside a vast windowless chamber rows of torches hung aslant from the walls and the coffered ceiling was blackened with smoke. On tiers of benches along either side, the Holy Brotherhood sat in their robes like a ghostly choir, the shadows of the tall, peaked hoods shifting and dancing in the uneven light. At the far end of the room, carved stone cruciforms flanked the upraised throne of the Grand Dragon. Kodak's robe was scarlet. In his right hand he held a golden statuette of the Sun-hurler poised on one foot, head thrust forward, the precious life-giving orb lifted behind his back by an outstretched arm. (The Dreamer remembered the crash of ninepins, the laughing bowlers in ancient beer commercials.)

After the ritual formality and uniform chanting of the presentation ceremony, the Exalted One raised the masking flap of his hood and revealed a surprisingly warm and friendly face. His eyes, sinister and snake-like when isolated behind the slitted openings in the anonymous cloth, seemed benign and understanding. The Grand Dragon beckoned for Buick to come forward, and the boy knelt on the step before the shaft-mounted throne.

While the Holy Brotherhood looked on in silence, the Grand Dragon whispered confidentially to Buick, embroidering his narrative of renegade harassment with an amount of skillful flattery and pausing occasionally for an avuncular smile to look straight into Buick's praise-brightened eyes. In the end, the boy proclaimed his allegiance to Kodak, his ardent voice audible throughout the hall.

"Amen," the Brotherhood chanted.

The Grand Dragon clapped his hands and called for the sacred vessels; a gong took up the summons; robed attendants passed through the room, filling the shallow metal bowls with wine; a hundred voices joined in common pledge. The Grand Dragon drank first. Buick reverently raised the holy dish to his lips. (*Hubcaps,* mused the Dreamer as he tasted the sour sacramental wine.)

"Par . . . ? Are you there, Par?" Omar Tarquille, the Syndicate Executive, crossed the patio of the Dreamer's house, a
scowl of consternation scrawled across his features like the
unskilled signature of an apprentice forger.

"No sign of him down below," puffed the Security Agent,
out-of-breath from the unaccustomed effort of walking in the
open air. "Any luck here?"

"No, not a trace." Tarquille stared at the flagstone terrace
where their rocketsled sat, tilted like an oversized silver top
beside the ornamental pond. "If he's not inside, we'll have to
search the woods."

The Security Agent grunted with displeasure. "What a
place to live; insects and snakes and what-all." The prospect
of tramping through the woods was enough to dampen any
man's enthusiasm. "Let's have a look in the house."

The two men approached the sealed entrance. The Security Agent tapped out a code-number on his portocall and
waited a few seconds while the machines back at headquarters ran through the classified files and located the combina-
tion to the Dreamer's house. He dialed the secret numbers
on the doorplate and the wide, circular entrance slid silently
open, expanding from the center like an iris. Only members
of the Security Agency were authorized to enter a citizen's
home without consent, and Tarquille waited outside while
the Agent stepped into the hall and asked the computer
where he could find Mr. Sondak.

"Mr. Sondak is not to be disturbed," the laconic voice answered.

"Is he alive?"

"His health is excellent."

"And where is he now?"

"In the studio . . . dreaming."

"Well, Mr. Tarquille," the Agent said, "looks like everything is in order here."

"Nonsense. No one stays hooked-up for a month, not even a Dreamer. I have a Committee order stating that I am to *see* Mr. Sondak, and I mean to see him and not be put off by some computer."

The arrangements were simple. The Agent took the computer's serial number and checked it with his portocall, receiving in return the code-coordinates for countermanding programmed instructions. A new program was written and the computer directed the two men down the metal corridor to the studio. They found Sondak sitting naked on the edge of the ovoid chamber, rubbing his eyes and scratching under his arm. "Why, Omar," he yawned, "what are you doing here?"

"No cause for alarm, Mr. Sondak. I'm Security Agent Justin Sattermeyer." He pointed to the golden disk on his service belt. "We're here with Executive Committee authorization. There's been some concern expressed regarding your whereabouts and the state of your health."

"Par, I've been trying to set up a conference with you for

almost a week. Naturally, I grew worried when all I could get out of your computer was that you were incommunicado."

Sondak shook his head. "How stupid of me. I should have left a message."

"Have you been dreaming all this time?" There was an anxious note in the Executive's voice.

"No. Sorry to disappoint you, Omar, but I've been conducting a little experiment. Desert exploration, you might call it. I was monitoring someone out there wired-up for D.E.M. transmission."

"You got to be careful, Mr. Sondak," Security Agent Sattermeyer said. "I had a friend working for Vicarious Heroics; he was monitoring a D.E.M. of a rocket race when the electron accelerator exploded. The ship went up like a star going nova. The pilot wearing the probe never knew what hit him. My friend never knew what hit him either. His heart couldn't take it. By the time they got to him it was too late for a transplant."

"That must have been years ago," Omar Tarquille said. "Dream-tables nowadays come equipped with an automatic safety cut-off."

"Yeah, but Mr. Sondak wasn't using his table, he was locked in there with those receptors strapped on his head."

"Well, I'm in good shape, as everyone can see," the Dreamer said, laughing as if he'd made a joke. "What did you want to confer with me about, Omar?"

"It's in the nature of a private matter . . ." Tarquille used his eyebrows like daggers but the Agent stood his ground, armored by a bored expression, oblivious to such subtleties. "If both parties are agreed," he said, "I'll wait outside. But you better both be alive when you're finished."

"Now, now, Mr. Sattermeyer, your profession has infected you with cynicism." The Dreamer stepped down and gave the Security Agent a friendly shoulder-pat, chuckling good-naturedly. "Omar and I are like Siamese-twins; we depend on each other for survival. I'm sure neither of us has any-thing to fear from the other." And Agent Sattermeyer was eased to the door with the nicest of smiles and a soft, wet handshake.

When the two men were alone, the Dreamer's expression changed. "I'm also certain that your explanation of all this will be amusing, Omar."

"I don't think you'll laugh," Tarquille replied with a knowing smirk. "Six days ago, the Committee voted to include dreams, hologramatics and D.E.M.s in the frequency-of-use quotas along with other commercial products. Under the terms of the new ruling, Par, all but fifty-seven of your dreams are being recalled from public circulation. I hate to think what your credit rating will look like unless you can come up with something better than your last vague effort."

"I stand chastened, Omar." The Dreamer's mocking smile never varied. "But, as the effort was mine, I can hardly understand the condemnation of a parasite who owes his existence to my toil." Sondak waved off the Executive's sputtered retort. This was the first time he had ever seen Omar Tarquille face-to-face, except for projection-booth conferences where the illusion of rural tranquility served to diffuse the hostility they felt toward one another. Here, in the closeness of his studio room, the mirrored walls multiplied their differences a hundred times. In a moment, they would be at each other's throats. Sondak broke the tension. "Spitting like cats isn't going to solve our problem. I do appreciate the seriousness of what you've told me, Omar."

"If only you had a new Dream ready to go."

"I may have considerably better than that. Let me put something interesting on the table for you. Can you spare two hours?"

Par Sondak led the way into the hall, evading the Executive's questions. He made his guest comfortable on the dream-table and, after consulting with the computer, played the section of the D.E.M. where Buick led the mounted warriors of the Grand Dragon into battle against the renegade Nomads.

The Dreamer waited in his library. Rather than spend the afternoon exchanging inanities with the Agent on the patio, he sent the serving-cart out with a tray of food and drink and retired to the sanctity of his books, leaving the guardian of his security gorging with both trotters in the trough. Reading was of no help; too much was at stake. Sondak sat, listlessly turning the pages of a folio edition of Hogarth's *Marriage à la Mode*, while the computer played Scarlatti.

When the announcement came that Omar Tarquille had awakened, the Dreamer asked the computer to direct him to the library. Prepared to be stoic in the face of bad news, Sondak was taken off guard by the Executive's enthusiastic entrance: "Par, it's incredible! Why, it's every bit as fantastic as one of your Dreams, with the immediacy of a D.E.M. You're a genius, Par. How did you ever think of it? I'll give you a Syndicate pledge for five years of credit . . . no, make it ten; ten years of credit for the market rights on this."

Sondak attempted to conceal his elation with a show of indifference. "Well . . . I hadn't thought. It's hard to set a price . . ."

"Nonsense! If I were dealt four aces, I'd play the hand, not sit back and admire my cards."

"All right. In that case, make it fifty years and it's yours."

"A little steep, Par, considering you'll still get your usual percentages; but, I'm willing to gamble. In fact, have your computer get the modes ready for an agreement."

"How about a drink to seal the bargain? I have some brandy here of which I'm quite proud."

Two glasses were filled; Omar Tarquille lifted his in salute. "To the incredible Buick," he said. The chime of touching crystal was echoed by the pealing clock. "I must be off, Par, the trajectory to the City takes at least an hour. To speed things up, why don't you transfer the Nomad's signal to the machines in my office. That would leave your studio free for dreaming, if the urge should strike you. In fact, it might be a good idea if you put all the modemat you've got on the waves to me right away; the sooner I get it, the sooner we can begin serialization."

"Don't you trust me with the mixing?"

"Par, why trouble yourself with technicalities? Leave the busy work to those without imagination. Take some time off and conjure up a good dream. After all, you've got fifty years to spare."

That night, Par Sondak was in no mood for the library. Reading was impossible. He couldn't concentrate. His mind skipped from line to line until he was skimming pages like a child pretending to be literate. The ticking of the clock drove him from the room. He started on a restless walk through the flower beds only to turn back abruptly to the house before he was gone ten minutes. By giving up his modes, the Dreamer could no longer regard the interlude with Buick in the light of scholarship. It ceased being an experiment the moment he transfered the signal to the City. He could still monitor the Nomad in his studio but he hesitated to admit, even to himself, that the boy had become such an obsession.

Only when he began considering the projection-booth as an alternative (holograms, the last refuge of the lonely) did he quit cursing Omar Tarquille for leaving him without an excuse and hurry to his studio.

This time, he made sure to record a message with the computer stating that he was on a two-month dream-holiday and would be unavailable for conferences. The intravenous feeding schedule was programmed and instructions were left with the clinic for his daily inoculations. A man with fifty years' credit could afford a little self-indulgence. In a few months, he would have to share Buick with a host of paying customers; but, for the time being, the public was uninvited. Par Sondak adjusted elastic straps and electrodes, slipping the crown of probe-receptors tightly onto his bald head before he climbed into the padded studio.

Buick leaned against a window-ledge and stared into the night through wrought iron scrollery that encircled the stars in its tendrils. On the parapet below, a silhouette stood guard by the shadowed disk of a great gong, ready to take up the alarm at the first sound of the watchtower bells. Buick drew the folds of his robe tighter about his chest, shivering in the chill air. He knew that in a very real sense these rooms were a prison; the guard outside was his jailer. In spite of the victory feasts and elegant words of praise, Buick no longer trusted the Grand Dragon. The charm and flattery did little to conceal the manipulations of court politics. His power strengthened Kodak's position and, for the moment, he was esteemed and honored. But the very nature of his strength made him a potential threat and Buick had heard enough of Brotherhood intrigue to know the fate of those who stood in the way of the Grand Dragon's ambition.

He must never relax his caution. He slept alone; the light-that-never-dies always ready in his hand. He bolted the heavy door to his rooms at night and was pleased with the thought that the same bars which kept him in also served to keep potential assassins safely out. Tomorrow, the servants who brought his meals would sample the food before he touched it. Kodak had his loyal tasters; why shouldn't the Firechief be accorded a similar honor? Before the morning was out, the entire Brotherhood would hear the story. What better way to serve the Grand Dragon notice that he was prepared for treachery?

The man lying on the ledge under the taut spread of camouflage netting paid no attention to the sunrise. He was not the sort to be distracted by natural beauty. His mind never strayed from the job at hand. That was the secret of his success. He wore a skin-tight, one-piece survival suit, the kind used in space, and by aquanauts, thousands of feet below the ocean surface. His lithe, muscular build suggested a man of action. In the center of his forehead swelled the slight subcutaneous bulge of an implanted mini-probe.

The man was busy with his equipment. He was a professional and didn't waste time. He adjusted the image on the portable viewscreen. It showed an empty stretch of road, three kilometers distant. No sign of his client yet. A turret-lens mounted in his orbiting rocketsled kept watch automatically. He checked the road below again through his magnascope. The angle was perfect, thirty-eight degrees. The range was seven-hundred meters. One of the minidisplays on his console showed a six kph increase in wind velocity, coupled with a twelve degree directional change from S-SW toward due South. The man checked these figures with his calculator and a new trajectory was plotted. The calibrated knobs on the telescopic sights were adjusted accordingly. At that moment, the viewscreen showed a lone rider approaching at a fast trot.

The man settled his shoulder comfortably behind the tripod mounted weapon and rested his cheek against the wooden stock, squinting through the 10x scope, but not yet touching the foregrip or the trigger. The strangest thing about this assignment was the weapon: a regular museum-piece. The man believed every assignment was strange in its own way. This was as close as he came to a philosophy. Either it was plastic surgery and play-acting, or he had to do something freakish, like use a knife or even his hands. It didn't matter. He would use a boomerang if the pay was right.

The antique ballistic weapon had been issued to him along with his instructions, but he took it in stride like a pro and spent two full days practicing on the desert until, at this range, he could put ten rounds cleanly through the center of a target and cover them all with a playing card. A glance at the viewscreen showed the client at the mouth of the canyon and the man double-checked the wind velocity. He rubbed his hands and waited, watching the bend in the road far below.

A rider came into sight. The cross-hairs in the scope centered on the red numbers on his shirt: 66. It was the client. The man inhaled, holding his breath as his finger bent around the trigger. A distant blunderbuss-boom of musketry brought his head up. ("Ambush?") His client's horse reared and went down, smoke rising like puffs of steam from the bushes on either side of the road. A viewscreen close-up showed the client thrown free, huddled against the belly of the dead horse, spots of blood beginning to blossom on the white tunic. Then: a dancing ribbon of flame; the boy had a solar-torch set at full power. The bushes along the roadside caught fire. "What kind of circus is this?" the man wondered.

"*Never mind,*" said an unfamiliar voice within his head. "*Finish him.*"

"What about the other ones?" the man was thinking.

"*Forget them. Just finish the job.*"

The man did as he was told.

There was a moment, sprawled in the dust, hurt and confused, when Par Sondak almost forced himself awake enough to push the disconnect sensor on the studio wall. Buick's instincts took over; surprise and fear cleared his mind of shock, and he crawled for the cover of the horse, his painful wounds only tinder for his incendiary hatred. Sondak shared the boy's furious energy and he postponed awakening like a man delaying an orgasm, wanting to taste just a little bit more of the thrill.

How satisfying to spray the underbrush with fire. The agonized screams of his enemies brought on a sensation almost like joy. Buick never heard the distant echoing shot that sent clouds of birds wheeling into flight from the sides of the canyon. A 250-grain, hollow-point bullet caught him under his upraised arm with enough force to flip him over backwards. Sondak felt the blow, saw a final rushing moment of blue sky; but when the body hit the ground, mouth and nostrils spewing a bright froth of lung-blood, the recording modal on the Dream Syndicate machines went blank and the Dreamer lay open-mouthed in his studio, his goggling eyes glassy with death.

The burial platform of Buick the Firechief was a banner-decked wagonwheel set on a mast above the uppermost ramparts of the fortress. And when the vultures finished, the bones were brought down and ceremoniously interred by the

Holy Brotherhood beneath the pavingstones of the Klaven Chamber. The Grand Dragon was bed-ridden with arthritis and did not attend these rites. Neither did five badly burned guardsmen, secretly hospitalized in an empty granary. The unrecognizably charred corpses of three renegade assassins hung from the crossbeam of the village gate.

Upended cinders, scorned even as carrion, the mortal remains of this doleful trio endured longer than the Grand Dragon or his fortress: a fire started mysteriously, deep within the inner chambers of the central keep, and spread with demonic ferocity, igniting the powder-magazines even as the first alarm gongs were sounding. For months afterwards, mothers pointed the three burned bodies out to their children as clear evidence of prophecy, a sign of unspeakable evil harbored within the massive smoke-blackened walls.

The picture-wall in Omar Tarquille's office throbbed with the programmed chaotics of Lazalo Kingsolving's *Sidereal Motion Series: Apparition 4.* On a pedestal in the center of the room stood one of the prizes of the Syndicate collection: Brancusi's *Bird in Space.* It was a large office in a world where status could be measured in square meters: the extent of one's wall-to-wall privacy. The view through the bubble-window opposite the entrance showed sergeant majors and queen angelfish gliding through a spiky forest of elkhorn coral. In the subsurface City, most of the population lived and worked at depths where, if they were fortunate enough to have an outer room, the only view was a hundred meters of dismal artificially lighted murk. His sunlit vista of the coral reef and the fact that he worked at home were other indications of Omar Tarquille's considerable power. The Security Agent on the dream-table had been impressed. Tarquille guessed it was his first assignment upstairs.

A tiny, tuning-fork hum woke the Agent. "Nomads?" he muttered. "Where'd you ever come up with an idea like that? You stand to make big points on this one, Mr. Tarquille."

The Executive dismissed the notion of personal gain with a careless wiggle of his fingers. "Hardly matters at the moment, I think. When I saw the report of Par's death I was astonished by the coincidence that it was precisely the same instant as the shooting of our Nomad. Precisely. That's why I got in touch with your Agency."

"And you say Mr. Sondak would sometimes monitor this transmission?"

"Frequently, I'm afraid. His own work wasn't going too well recently."

"I know, I had to sleep through all that unfinished stuff of his: pretty sad. We had it marked down as suicide; you knew his credit-rating was shot to hell, of course. We figured he'd worked out some tricky way of using the studio to have it look like a natural death. But, your theory makes just as much sense, Mr. Tarquille."

"That's very gratifying to hear, especially if it clears up any clouds which have gathered around my friend's name. Par Sondak was a great artist and should be remembered as such."

"I understand the Committee is having his library moved intact to the Public Reading Room as a memorial."

"Yes, except the Velazquez and the Turner watercolors go to the Committee Board Room." Omar Tarquille had looked into the angles involved, but the regulations were clear: all of a dead man's remaining credit and assets revert to the common trust. Committee members always plucked the choicest plums in the name of civic improvement. "I don't know what the plans for the house are," he said, "but it will be a long time before anyone has enough credit for a place like that again."

"Oh, I don't know, Mr. Tarquille," the Security Agent said with a smile like a piece of bread buttered on both sides. "I expect you'll be moving in yourself after you release these Nomad modes."

Again, the shrug of wiggled fingers. "Not a chance. You won't catch me out in that wilderness, I'm too fond of people."

"Anyone with eyes can see that you are, Mr. Tarquille."

The Agent's amiable chuckle resembled the eager panting of a poodle playing fetch. "You like people and people like you, and that's a plain fact if there ever was one."

The Executive's answering smile was a masterpiece of facial engineering. He pressed a sensor on the control panel and a pretty Syndicate hostess appeared to show the Security Agent to the door.

END

HOMECOMING

THE AMBASSADORS glimmer, drifting through space like luminous snowflakes toward the mother planet. The gradual transition from a state of pure energy accelerates their ever-shifting geometry. Shape and color alter kaleidoscopically in the long glide to the surface. Alone in the endless night, the home colony awaits their return.

❖

The crystal planet is iridescent. Every facet of the angular, prismatic surface glows from within. No moons orbit this singular treasure. The nearest sun-star is a trillion miles distant. At the hub of the universe a vivid jewel pulses with life.

❖

Witness the birth-spasms of the ambassadors: surface crystals gather light with intensifying brilliance until they energize and are gone, spread like invisible spore in a fluid rush across the curve of time. A haphazard trajectory carries them through the distant void. The possibilities of their eventual return are merely theoretical.

❖

The colony exists as a single organism. The planet is alive to its core: billions upon billions of individual crystalline forms interlinked and cloning, united in a structure that shares a single intelligence.

❖

Reaching the surface, the ambassadors bond with the mother planet, merging their private chemistries with the ruling order of the colony. The reunion is total bliss. An instant of joy spans the antipodes. The colony is one again. It is as if every crystal in the planet's structure has blazed new trails across the universe.

❖

An ambassador's return is always the cause of some regret. So many of the planets encountered in the eternal drift of space are dead. Most are stillborn; sterile rock piles forever silent. Saddest are the cold, bleached skeletons of once-flourishing bio-cultures. The life-impulse is nourished through contact with other living worlds and the discovery of so much death is discouraging. Only positive memories stimulate the plural unconscious of the colony.

❖

On one forlorn planet fire-storms swept a desert of ashes and cinders. Clinging to the black glassy slopes of obsidian mountains, a species of disk-shaped, leather-textured lichenoids was all that remained of life. The planet was number nine in a solar-system of twenty-four: all dead. The problem and the solution were simple. Certain trace elements of helium were lacking in the atmosphere. A minor correction. The ambassador adjusted the chemistry of the planet and continued on through space.

❖

It is the occasional return of her ambassadors that reaffirms the colony's function in the cycle of creation. This is the only measure of the mother planet's success. How many bright diplomats have never come back, energy-impulses lost forever among the wheeling galaxies? How many distant planets owe the gift of life to the undetected manipulations of a passing ambassador? When life hangs in the balance the slightest gesture tips the scales: specific gravity altered by a fraction, a chance mutation, an addition to the periodic table. Such miracles are automatic for an ambassador.

❖

The greatest victory for the home colony is the preservation of highly advanced life-forms. It is rare for mature bio-cultures to require assistance but even the most developed mechanism is susceptible to the unexpected. One small blue-green planet, the third in a solar-system of nine, supported an incredible variety of living organisms. Almost totally aqueous, its most perfectly evolved species were oceanic. Even terrestrial life had originally come out of the surrounding seas. Yet, one aberrant land creature, unable to exist in harmony with its neighbors, had created an artificial environment that so poisoned the oceans and atmosphere that the planet was tipping into the abyss of extinction. Less than one-hundred solar-years of life remained.

❖

The ambassador's solution was inspired. Overpopulation made the offending biped particularly vulnerable to infection and a modest viral mutation soon eliminated the problem. No other species was affected. Now the little planet prospers. The mother colony shares a final vision: large schools of the predominant life-form spouting on the wave-tossed surface of the bountiful sea. A contented glow emanates from within the crystal planet.

THE CLONE
WHO RAN FOR CONGRESS

A DOZEN YEARS AGO, during my first season in corporate sports, I was one of fifty image modifiers working shifts at Syndicated Athletics. Our department redesigned the features and biographical data of contracted athletes who, although they had fallen considerably in viewer popularity, were not yet sufficiently burned-out to be retired. The job requires a high degree of skill and training, yet even plastic surgeons earn more.

Too poor at the time to afford the cheapest house clone, I lived a fair distance out in the city's lake district in a two-room automated apartment with a closet-sized Holorama. I rode the public glide to work each morning in the company of computer programmers and junior-grade statisticians. Recycled hi-pro for breakfast, a window-seat on the glide, streets silent save for the methodical gray-clad army of clones sweeping and collecting garbage.

I worked all morning on a series of portrait sketches for the surgical department. I was redesigning an affable red-haired Irish third baseman who had recently slipped in the ratings. In a couple of months, he would reappear in the ballpark as a dark and surly Cuban outfielder. Strictly a routine modification.

Near the end of my shift our section chief rang for attention. We had a visiting executive: a florid gentleman whose robust form bespoke a diet of meat; no more powdered food once you attain executive status. He made a speech about clones. His rich, deep voice boomed with energy and enthusiasm. He waved his arms in small circles like a man in a balancing act.

"Mankind has been forever freed from drudgery," he exulted. "All of the hateful, menial jobs which plagued our ancestors have been assumed by these efficient, single-minded laborers. It's miraculous! Chromosome control enables us to design the worker to fit the task. Unlimited numbers of identical twins! Biotechnology! Genetic engineering! The possibilities are limitless."

The executive rubbed his hands and glanced around the office. "Our beloved Chairman," he murmured, a plump hand fluttering to rest over his heart, "has taken a bold, innovative step destined to revolutionize the sports industry. Our bio-labs have engineered the perfect athlete. Yesterday's dreams become the products of today." The executive snapped his fingers and his assistant flung open the office door. A beetle-browed giant lumbered inside.

The executive beamed. "Prototype number 916 is a triumph of bioengineering, a physiologically perfect athlete. He is the matrix of our new sports system. From one cell we have cloned thousands of mirror twins. Currently, they are undergoing specialized training. Very soon, entire teams of identical players will take the field against our rivals. I guarantee one thing, gentlemen: Syndicated Athletics has forever altered the history of corporate sports."

Our section chief led the applause as the entire department stood and sang the company anthem. The executive joined in on the chorus. Prototype 916 hummed along tunelessly, shuffling and blinking, his clonish features inert.

The executive held up his hands to quiet our cheering. "It is a great moment for Syndicated. But our work is just beginning. If 916 is as successful as predictions indicate, it won't be very long before our competition comes up with similar models of their own. We've got the jump on them in any case. Even with the accelerated hormone treatment, it takes ten years to bring a clone to maturity. By the time Trans Am or ProSports produces clones of their own, our champ here will have a new image."

He clumped the docile giant on the back. "Not much in looks or personality. Not until you modifiers do your stuff. We want an athlete with audience appeal, an image that will go straight to their hearts. Syndicated is opening this assignment to competition. Great things are in store for the modifier who clicks with the winning image."

The executive gave the company salute and left. The

clone didn't move, hulking slack-jawed before us until the executive assistant took him by the arm and ushered him gently out.

There were some smiles in the department, but nobody actually laughed. When the shift ended, I headed straight for the company library. For several months, my schedule never varied; after four hours on the job, I'd spend the following two shifts doing research in the library. I wasn't alone. Half the department scrambled among the microfilm racks like graduate students.

Syndicated Athletics declared a company holiday the day we unleashed the world's first all-clone team. Fleets of private glides ferried the employees out to a special section in the stadium. I had not seen live football since university days and thrilled to a thousand forgotten sensations, all the nuance of sound and smell and weather lacking on Holorama. Of course, "Holorama puts *you* in the action," and from where I was sitting, not even my neighbor's binoculars were much help on that score. Too far to observe the stunned reactions of the opposition when the Silver Warriors, Syndicated's new team, took the field. The Phantom Freebooters of ProSports Ltd were one of the original Victory League teams, but even players long accustomed to dramatic image changes in the lineup were unprepared for this phalanx of clones.

Those interested in a description of the game are better off dialing a Holorama replay. The Silver Warriors won; not by much, and certainly not due to any invincible clone skill, but merely because the players were interchangeable and identical replacements unlimited. The typical technological triumph.

Within weeks, all of Syndicated's teams were manned by clones, although there were no further holidays. Inexorable as ants, victory piled on victory, yet curiously, our ratings declined. The fans weren't happy. Instead of an ever-changing multitude of stars there was only stolid number 916 to receive their cheers. Whatever the sport, Syndicated's team consisted of one player, infinitely repeated like a reflection in a hall of mirrors. The surgical department worked over-time to provide variety, performing hundreds of nose-jobs and face-lifts, but the problem was more than cosmetic. No matter how you sliced it, prototype 916 had less appeal than a boiled potato.

Image mod had been handed the ball. There were daily executive pep talks and a credit bonus was added to up the ante. I knew my colleagues had access to the same material from the Golden Age of professional sports (bubblegum trad-ing cards, comic books, fan magazines, paperbacks), and my strategy anticipated a host of familiar images: Micky Mantle, Muhammad Ali, Joe Namath; all careers resurrected with regularity. I concentrated my research instead on an earlier and more innocent time, the turn of the Twentieth Century.

Popular literature of the period took the form of "dime novels," crude, mass-produced pamphlets. I read hundreds on microfilm before my diligence was rewarded. Within the yellowed pages of the *Tip Top Weekly*, "An ideal publication for the American Youth," I found the image I was after: Frank Merriwell, a Yale college football and baseball hero.

Fans today knew only heroics without chivalry. A team composed of identically perfect gentlemen seemed designed to go "straight to their hearts." I worked all week finishing the personality profiles, bioenergy patterns and full sets of sketches, leaving immediately on a three-day holiday without pay after submitting my proposal in the morning.

The sub-continental glide brought me straight from Bermuda and I entered the office refreshed by one last swim before work. I had transferred to an afternoon shift and when I reported, my new section chief told me I had an appointment with an executive upstairs. My heartbeat led the way like a drummer as I rode the tube to the ninetieth floor. I gave my name and was escorted, oblivious to the startling beauty of the attendant, into a sanctuary of cool marble columns and tranquil reflecting pools.

Most of it was on Holorama. Executive offices stay tuned to a private channel and unlimited surroundings are available to suit the occupant's mood. This executive greeted me dressed in a toga. He reclined on a low couch beside a table heaped with fruit and dainty sweetmeats. These were real and quite delicious. A drink arrived while hologram peacocks paraded around us. The executive said a brilliant career lay ahead of me. "The bonus is yours, of course, but that's only the beginning. Your future is linked to your remarkable image. What a stroke of genius! An athlete pure in mind and deed; brave, loyal, courteous. The fans will adore him!"

I mumbled my gratitude to the company, but he went on as if I were not even there.

"Only one serious rival out of hundreds of submissions. Came from a modifier on the third shift. He found this marvelous comic book hero, an English Lord who lives like a naked savage among the apes in Africa."

"Tarzan."

"That's it. You do know your stuff, don't you? The selection committee felt this ape man's background was too elitist for popular taste; a mid-western farmboy raised by wolves would be more to the point. Your contribution, dear lad, is inspirational. You've been promoted to the rank of associate executive. A new team, the Royal Hunters, has been designated for your image. You are the sole company spokesman and publicist for that team. Our bio-labs are formulating the required genetics. Education and conditioning will determine this clone's eventual personality. Your first assignment is to take charge of training and prototype development. He's your baby now."

Every detail had to be pre-planned. Working with a team of company neurologists, I designed a program of prenatal stimuli. Psychologists were consulted on plans to update the standard nursery facilities. Executive privilege includes the use of a company four-seater glide and a month after implementation I took a hop out to our suburban bio-labs.

White-gowned and gloved, I inspected the laboratory's gestation facilities, escorted by an equally beshrouded section chief. Like a pair of ghosts, moving soundlessly on sterile rubber slippers, voices muffled by mask-like viral filters, we toured the cloning trays and fertilization tanks. The embryos, hundreds of them, floated like aquatic cherubs in individual jars of amniotic fluid.

"Royal Hunter One." The section chief pointed to the first fetus in line. "The matrix for the entire series."

"And the gestation period is three months?"

"Eighty-two days precisely. Decanting is followed by a period of phenomenal growth which lasts another six months. At that age, the clone resembles a five-year-old human in terms of physical development, and the growth rate, although still accelerated, levels off for the next nine-and-a-half years."

The prenatal stimulation sequence was going according to plan and I asked my guide for a progress report on the incubation nurseries designed to house the clones for the six crucial months after decanting.

"They're ready now." The section chief led the way into a neighboring chamber where ranks of glass-walled nurseries stood along the walls. "Every unit is individually temperature and humidity controlled," he said as we passed down the line, peering through the glass like window-shoppers. Red rubber balls waited in each compartment. Band music and cheering crowds played continuously in the background. Even the air was artificially scented with the aroma of sweat and liniment.

The nursling's rapid physical development gave everyone attached to the Royal Hunter project a particular sense of urgency. During the six months of incubation, I had crews of construction clones working round the clock at one of Syndicated's training farms in the south. Stone by weathered stone, these zombie laborers pieced together an exact reproduction of a New England prep school, circa 1885. Leaded glass panes in the gabled windows, copper weather vanes high above mossy slate rooftops, granite porch steps scalloped by time: not one detail was overlooked.

Half-an-hour before the convocation ceremonies, clone gardeners hurriedly hung ivy on the brick walls, stopping only for our Chairman's engrossing speech. The Royal Hunters, proper schoolboys now in their neat blue blazers and striped beanies, stood in perfect formation on the quad. To conclude the official ceremony, 1000 boyish soprano voices joined in singing the school's alma mater, a stirring martial melody as familiar to them as their own heartbeats after three months of continuous play in the nursery.

There followed a nine-year career as headmaster of Royal Hunter Hall. I kept my office at company headquarters, but aside from a monthly visit, the Holorama remained disconnected and the bare, windowless chamber must have seemed bleak even to the custodial clones. My new office on the third floor of the Hall was a pleasant Victorian study with walls of leatherbound books, several Chinese urns sporting palms and a carved oak desk; quite comfortable considering the decor couldn't be changed by turning a dial.

No Holorama was permitted at the school. Transportation was by bicycle only. The nearest glide terminal stood several miles distant from campus. Every effort had been made to shield the boys (I could never think of my charges as "clones") from the realities of present-day America. The leisurely life-tempo at Royal Hunter Hall encouraged courtesy and a sense of grace.

The classes were rigidly old-fashioned. The boys studied ethics, hygiene, ancient history, the classics, as well as elementary math and literature. Daily chapel attendance was compulsory; the library well-stocked with uplifting volumes. Athletics comprised most of the school's curriculum. My office windows overlooked the playing fields, the boys in their whites moving in perfect precision across the even green lawn. Intramural games started early in the morning and continued noisily until dark. Sprinters and hurdlers and long-distance runners pranced like thoroughbreds on the track. The soft thud of the 16-pound shot was continuous, like an iron rainfall.

The boys could be distinguished on the field by the numbers marking their jerseys. This was somewhat more difficult in the classrooms, where small numerical pins worn on blazer lapels were all that differentiated Royal Hunter 12 from Royal Hunter 367. My own duties as administrator were greatly simplified by the uniformity of my charges. To gauge student opinion, I arranged meetings with various boys selected at random from among the school's population. The answers I received were as interchangeable as the mirror images offering them. In time, I came to rely upon a single student as an accurate reflection of group attitudes. This was Royal Hunter One, the matrix of the system. I called him Roy.

Over the few short years of his accelerated growth, I grew quite fond of Roy Hunter. Certainly, he (along with his 999 twin siblings) was a lad any father would happily call his own. Brave, courteous and loyal, ever ready to extend a hand to a fallen opponent, Roy brightened even the foulest of my moods with his perpetually cheerful smile and impeccable manners. Our prep school was a charade, a figment of corporate athletics, but a utopian atmosphere of decency and sportsmanship evolved and in the end I succumbed to it,

along with my entire faculty of hand-picked psycho-thera-
pists.

My monthly sojourns to company headquarters became a
matter of hours rather than days. I would have avoided the
office altogether but for the required report to the board. Syndicated's monopoly on all-clone teams lasted less than five
seasons. Within a year, both Trans Am and ProSports sent
their own Neanderthal prototypes thundering out onto the
playing fields of America. Corporate sports fell into a slump
in spite of the expensive promotion touting clone athletes as
perfect for Holorama.

Board meetings, never frivolous affairs at best, came to
resemble mortician's conventions. The formal solemnity
seemed but a step away from outright despair. When the
Royal Hunter boys attained full growth at eight years, there
was considerable corporate pressure to start them immediately in professional competition. I resisted with the bland
assurances of a politician wiggling out of a campaign promise. I wanted to play Mr. Chips just a little bit longer on my
make-believe campus.

The first time I heard Roy Hunter mention the Olympics
was in the spring of that last year. We were having one of our
regular chats in my study, tea and biscuits before a glowing
fire. Roy held his delicate bone china cup with a grace that
belied the awesome strength in his hands. I remember his
pleasant smile and the golden shine of his curls in the fire-
light. We spoke of sports and I asked which was his favorite.

"The decathlon," he said without hesitation.

"Really? Not football or baseball?"

Roy balanced his cup on his knee. "I don't mean to sound like a snob, sir. Football's quite a lot of fun, but it's only a game."

"Only a game?"

"From the corporate viewpoint I guess it's an industry," he blushed, "but out on the field it's still a game."

"And what about the spirit of competition?"

"Oh, it's there, of course." The boy stared deep into the fire like an augur sorting the truth from among the dancing flames. "Team spirit is a wonderful thing, but individual competition demands a greater inner resource. The classic track and field events have challenged the human spirit for millennia, all the way back to the ancient Greeks. The Greeks dated their calendar from the time of the first Olympiad, that's how important they thought it was."

Perhaps it was a gleam of reflected fire-light, but as he spoke his eyes glowed with a fervor I had never before detected.

The teacup rattled in his hand, a seismograph of his violent emotions.

"Olympic Standard Time?" I chuckled, hoping a joke would defuse the sudden tension.

He hadn't heard me and went on as if possessed. "Wars would stop during the month of Olympic competition. Athletics were sacred to the Greeks. They were more than just games. Olympia was holy ground. The famous sculptor, Phidias, kept a workshop there and . . . and his statue of Zeus in the temple at Olympia was one of the Seven Wonders of the World. It was over forty feet tall!"

A long silence punctuated by the snapping fire ended when Roy shrugged and set his cup on the table beside him. "Sorry I got so carried away, sir."

What surprised me was the passion of his outburst. After ten years perfecting the Royal Hunter image, this was the first indication I'd had of any deeply held convictions on the boy's part. He had been taught from the moment of conception to love sports, but I never intended to create a fanatic. I reached over and patted his shoulder. "Nothing to fret about," I said. "It's only natural you should have strong feelings about athletics."

"They're my whole life," he blurted. "Nothing else matters."

A week or so later, standing at the edge of the sawdust pit on the playing field, Roy's fervent words echoed in the private corridors of my mind. Several boys were practicing the long jump and the trainers marked each effort with a steel tape. All about me javelins pierced the air, spiked feet danced on the surrounding ribbon of cinder track, pole vaulters catapulted aloft, shot and hammer thumped into the soft earth.

Roy's self-assured movements as he prepared to jump prompted the thought that the number on his shirt, the numeral one, was instead a pronoun, advertising his individuality in the first person singular. He smiled and began his approach, running with such fluid elegance that his takeoff at the board seemed an effortless continuation into flight. It was more a defiance of gravity than a jump, as beautiful a thing to watch as the soaring of a hawk.

"10.36 meters," the trainer with the tape called, kneeling beside Roy in the sawdust. "If this were an official meet, that would be the new world's record."

I shook the boy's hand and muttered something fatuous about keeping up the effort. He smiled, his chest heaving under his thin shirt. "Too bad we can't compete," he said. "They'd have to rewrite all the record books."

Roy was right. A cursory check in the library revealed the world's long jump record to be a hair over nine meters. The following week I carried the record book with me on the practice fields. Roy and his classmates made a lie out of every statistic. They did so with such regularity there was soon no point in thumbing the dog-eared pages.

I brought the record book to my next board meeting. Compared to executive offices with unlimited exotic surroundings available on Holorama, the board room at Syndicated Athletics was an austere chamber, muffled by darkness. A polished mahogany table stood enclosed within an oval island of light. The Chairman sat at the head with the members ranked down each side.

I read from the well-worn book with the glib assurance of an auctioneer. To a man, the board expressed delight hearing of Roy Hunter's record-breaking, further reaffirmation of their decision to go "all clone" a decade before. I complimented the board's foresight and mentioned, as if in passing, that it seemed a pity not to allow the boys to compete. "Any victories they win as amateurs will enhance their reputations as professionals. You couldn't buy better publicity."

Our Chairman leaned forward, stroking his square-cut beard, his voice a whisper crisp as the rustle of banknotes. "Have you given any thought to the sort of amateur competition that would guarantee the most exposure?"

"Yes, sir, I have."

"Out with it, man."

"The Olympic Games, sir."

That was the prod that set the ant hill stirring. The entire board spoke at once, a cacophonous intermingling of approval, denunciation, epithets and incredulity building in volume until our Chairman's conspicuous silence provided a contrast so profound that the uproar was lost within it. All fifteen members covered their embarrassment in a murmured spasm of quiet coughing.

"The Olympics are perfect," our Chairman whispered. "Start out straight at the top. We'll send one of our boys to the summer games in New Paris, cover him with gold medals so the public will have a new hero-image to worship and then, *boom*, introduce the Royal Hunters at the start of the fall football season."

And that's just the way it happened, more or less. The board agreed unanimously on the wisdom of having a single representative at the games, "to clearly focus the image in the public mind," and my choice went without hesitation to Roy. Final elimination trials for the U.S. team were held in April at National Stadium and Roy showed up at the qualifying rounds without having previously entered a meet and took first in six events. I instructed him to hold back a bit and so no records were set.

Everything proceeded according to plan until someone leaked Roy's connection with Syndicated Athletics to the media. There was talk of spies from the competition, but I've always suspected our whispering Chairman.

The IOC kicked Roy off the team on the grounds of "professionalism," but Syndicated's legal staff stood ready with a barrage of briefs and within a week obtained an injunction against the Olympic Committee. A district court judge ruled that Roy, as the "property" of Syndicated Athletics, could not be a "professional" because he received no compensation for his services.

"The cat is out of the bag," our Chairman said, looking very much like a cat himself as he stroked his whiskers at the head of the table. "I think it would be a good idea to take a bunch of the boys, say fifty or so, over to New Paris when you go. Since we've lost the element of surprise, we want to keep the Royal Hunter's team image before the public as much as possible."

A "good idea" from our Chairman is tantamount to a command and when Roy left for France on the Intercontinental, fifty of his mirror-twin siblings and I followed three days later in a private company glide. Viewers first saw us all together on "Holorama Hilites," posed as if for a class picture in our blazers and scarves under the pellucid Mediterranean sky. New Paris is a charming city of parks and monuments, seemingly designed for a succession of wreath-laying pilgrimages, and the Royal Hunters made numerous public appearances during the festivities.

Seeing the international art treasures assembled like jewels in this tiny nation's crown makes it difficult to imagine the world-wide outrage which greeted their purchase and removal at the turn of the century. We didn't miss a thing, from the weathered sandstone Sphinx on the Boulevard Egyptian to Winchester Cathedral in the Bois Central. The boys' favorite was the monumental Borglum sculpture of four early American presidents, originally hewn from a mountaintop in the Dakotas, and now rising like sea gods above the tranquil surface of the circular Lac de Liberté. Perhaps you watched us on Holorama, singing a patriotic Independence Day medley as fireworks blossomed over the shimmering reflections.

The same glorious Fourth marked the opening ceremonies of the XXXV Olympic Games at the Palais du Sport, a marble fantasy built from the splendid Roman ruins at Baalbec. The international athletes paraded under a triumphal arch as whirling clouds of pigeons rose skyward from among white rows of Corinthian columns. An estimated global Holorama audience of over a billion witnessed the lighting of the symbolic flame.

That audience more than doubled the next morning at the start of competition and continued to grow, day by day, as the tally of Roy's victories mounted. The odds are favorable that somewhere along the line you were in a Holorama watching Roy bow his head to receive yet another gold medal. "The Star-Spangled Banner" was replayed with such frequency it came to sound like theme-music.

For the first few days it seemed like a beautiful dream. Each victory was a private miracle. Roy took a gold in the pole vault, the long jump, the 100, 200 and 400 meter dashes, the 110 and 400 meter hurdles and the javelin. When the decathlon started on the fourth day Roy Hunter was the undisputed favorite.

I had a field pass and shuttled back and forth between my seat in the stadium with the rest of the Royal Hunter boys and a spot on the sidelines among various officials and media representatives. Not even Holorama gets you any closer to the action. Roy was an easy winner in the 100 meter dash, the first of the decathlon events. The long jump was next and I paced up and down behind the judges remembering an afternoon back at school when Roy set a world record. He broke it in New Paris with an approach like an ascending angel and a leap of such violence that he gashed his ankle with his spikes on the way down.

The shotput followed early in the afternoon with Roy dominating the field once again. In spite of the accustomed triumph something troubled me, something mysteriously wrong. During the high jump I figured out just what it was.

I caught up with Roy in the passageway under the stadium as he headed for the dressing rooms. "Great jump," I said, pacing at his side.

He grinned modestly. "I gave it my best shot."

"Don't undersell yourself, it was terrific. Especially considering you've got an injured foot."

Roy paused and brushed back a tousled forelock. "It's nothing, really."

"For once I'm inclined to believe you, Roy. It may be nothing now, but it was a nasty gash at the time. I saw it happen. You had it bandaged before the shotput. Only one problem: it was your right foot that got cut, but you're wearing the bandage on your left."

Roy glanced at the white dressing on his ankle, his boyish grin undiminished. "Go ahead," I told him, "take it off. Show me the wound and prove I was mistaken."

"The mistake was mine," Roy said, peeling back the bandage to reveal an ankle innocent of any injury.

"Not even a clone heals that fast," I said. "How many of you are in on this?"

"We're all in on it, sir."

"A different Roy Hunter competing in each event?"

"That's right, sir."

"And each of you has trained exclusively in his specialty?" The last piece of the puzzle slid into place.

"Of course."

"And this deception is your idea of fair play? Sneaking about switching costumes after you've entered all the events as an individual?"

"But, we are an individual, sir," Roy said, looking me straight in the eye. "We always have been. The notion of telling us apart with numbers seemed a joke; we always swapped our shirts and pins around at random. You were the only one who made a distinction."

"And all the chats I had with Roy in my study . . . ?"

"We took turns for that. As a unit, I was only in your office once. We talked about Jim Thorpe." The clone bent down and slapped the bandage he was holding into place on his right ankle. "Just think of us all as Roy," he said, sauntering off toward the showers. "That's who we are, of course. They are me and I am them."

The Royal Hunters went on to win the gold medal in the

decathlon, and in every other track and field event at New Paris. Twenty-four medals in all. Took turns wearing them, no doubt. Whichever one received the special trophy from the president had them all around his neck at once, like a 24-carat lei.

Why should I tell you this when you've seen it all on Holorama? The Royal Hunters are probably your favorite football team. For all I know, you even voted for him when he ran in your district. The nation loves a sports hero. It was clever of Roy to run simultaneously in every congressional district in the country. And downright sporting of the Supreme Court to let him/them do it. They tell me the visitor's gallery in the House of Representatives is jammed for every session now, but did you ever stop to think just who it was that got buried in that landslide victory?

GRAY MATTERS

The will to a system is a lack of integrity.

—

F. NIETZSCHE
The Twilight of the Idols

1. Hive

THE SCANNER SEES: unending gun-metal walls; waxed plastic flooring; three deHartzman Communicators, multifrequency channel finders attached and blinking; and the forward end of the subdistrict memory-file. A soft flush of lavender suffuses the luminous egg-crate ceiling, the first gentle trace of a dawning day. At the end of the aisle, the Sector's community power unit hums with life.

Next to the power unit, in the foremost deposit drawer, a solitary cerebromorph has switched off his scanner and floats in voluntary darkness. His number is A-0001-M(637-05-99). His name was Denton "Skeets" Kalbfleischer. Skeets is the oldest resident of the Depository. He is twelve years old and will remain so forever.

Over in Aisle B, an Amco-pak Mark IX maintenance van prowls silently along on pneumatic treads. The Mark IX is a clumsy piece of equipment and inventorial considerations alone keep it from becoming obsolete. Accordingly, its use is restricted to those Sectors established before the Awakening. Maintenance vans are programmed to perform a wide range of mundane chores: the Mark Is clean and polish the aisles each night, the Mark IIIs tend the power units. Every Amco-pak above Mark V is a mechanic, equipped with telescoping arms and lubricated digits capable of the most intricate and precise manipulations. Mechanically minded Depository residents never tire of watching the vans at work and a special scanner channel has been provided to satisfy these vicarious repairmen.

One Aisle B resident with no interest in the Amco-pak is a former Czechoslovakian motion-picture star housed in deposit drawer number B-0486-F(098-76-04). Classified female (in the advanced Sectors no sex distinctions are made between resident cerebromorphs), Vera Mitlovic spends her time screening old films. Although Center Control considers twentieth-century cinema frivolous, and thus detrimental to spiritual growth, the old movies are recorded in the memory bank and all Vera need do is check her Micro Index and dial the appropriate code key on the telescript console.

Vera is awake this morning before reveille serenade (today the overture to Wagner's *Der Fliegende Holländer*) and dials her first film the moment the memory bank librarian switches on for the day. (The film is *Bohemian Idyl*, a Czech romantic comedy, starring Vera as a Prague fashion designer who falls in love with a gypsy.) Three Center Control regulations for members of her category are neglected. By not checking her memo for a dream playback, she is unable to file the required auditing report; more importantly, for the third day in a row she misses the morning meditation exercise.

But Vera doesn't care. With the old film flickering, she is transported beyond the demands of Center Control. Does it matter if the print is in poor condition, the celluloid yellow and scratched? It is like watching her own ghost. The challis skirt lifts and swirls; her long limber legs gleam with firelight; she dances about the caravan encampment, tempting the fiddlers with her buoyant breasts. And where were those lovely legs today, those youthful breasts? Gone to dust with only their image preserved, a shadow etched in silver nitrate. Vera's joy is tinged with sadness and regret. If only she had eyes she would be weeping.

Two drawers down from where Vera views her melancholy matinee, Obu Itubi, a late twenty-second-century Nigerian sculptor (the most distinguished member of the school now known as the African Renaissance), programs a memory-bank entomology file on the habits of bees. Itubi's work with plastic and steel represents the final flowering of Western humanism, a last gasp of anthropomorphism before the machines lulled the world into meditation. His file number is B-0489-M(773-22-99).

The Amco-pak in Aisle B has finished its work on the auxiliary power unit. A malfunctioning valve has been located and replaced and the Mark IX sorts and repacks the complex array of tools laid out for the job. A comic business. The Amco-pak is an absent-minded octopus, searching with its many arms for a variety of misplaced gadgets. Scanner viewers are always amused by this clumsy clean-up operation.

The Amco-pak locates the tools and lumbers up the aisle, retractable arms stored, steel digits at rest, mindlessly treading toward its next assignment. Many Depository residents are frankly envious. They feel it a waste to bestow those miraculous fingers on a machine incapable of appreciating their worth.

Skeets Kalbfleischer is sleeping late; the reveille serenade digested into his dream, a stirring soundtrack for the Hollywood sex fantasies which still occupy his adolescent mind even after a four-hundred-year absence from Grade B double features. Skeets is a definite problem for Center Control. Because of his stature as a historic landmark, the very first cerebromorph and cornerstone of the oldest Depository in the System, his complete failure to achieve any measure of spiritual progress in this enlightened age following the awakening is a matter of considerable concern to the Auditing Commission.

The problem isn't that Skeets is not educated. In the years, decades, and centuries following his operation, Skeets has earned the equivalent of several dozen baccalaureate degrees. He has ten doctorates to his credit. Sealed in his cranial container from the age of twelve, Skeets has been spoon-fed knowledge by whole committees of curious scientists. Skeets is versed in mathematics, languages, the arts; he is an outstanding authority on molecular biology and ninth-century Indian cave painting. Learning, programmed on endless microfiles, has saturated his brain cells and Skeets spouts answers with the speed and accuracy of a computer. Denton Kalbfleischer is a very successful experiment. Only one problem: in this sophisticated age of meditation and spiritual liberation, Skeets still wants to be a cowboy.

". . . the superfamily *Apoidea*, consisting of various social and solitary hymenopterous insects. Observe *Apis mellifera*, the common honeybee, both industrious and social. This insect lives in a swarm consisting of three classes. The majority of the swarm are neuters, known commonly as workers; they gather the pollen and build the comb. The female is called the Queen; she is the reproducer, the egg layer, and there is only one per swarm. The male of the species is the drone and his is an idle life. The drone's only function is to. . . ." Obu Itubi isn't listening to the narrator's voice. He has turned the volume down until the mechanized monotone drawl is a murmur faint as the distant humming of the bees. All the more recent memory-files are narrated by computer and the soundtracks have an assembly-line sameness that makes Obu Itubi's flesh crawl. An unpleasant sensation, akin to the phantom pain amputees of an earlier age suffered in their missing limbs, for Itubi no longer has flesh.

A bower of evening primroses arches delicately over the lovers' heads, sweetly scenting the late afternoon. (They were made of paper and dusty from long storage in the property shop.) The slanting rays of an amber sunset gild the features of the handsome young couple. (The lightman was malicious and had trained his thousand-watt instruments directly into Vera's eyes.) Distant violins blend with the shimmering nocturne of nightingales and crickets. (The musicians were drunk and made rude remarks concerning the leading lady's private life. The bird calls and insect noises were produced by a fat pockmarked man who whistled into a microphone and rubbed two rosin-covered sticks.) "My beloved . . . my treasure . . ." the dark-eyed gypsy croons, while the blushing girl flutters and sighs. (His breath stank of garlic sausage and not even a heavy application of gum arabic kept his toupee from slipping slightly askew.) "Come away with me to the Moravian mountains, my love. I want to take you to the little village where I was born." (The leading man, who spoke Czech with a thick Slavic accent, was actually born in Croatia.) Leaning forward, he cups her radiant face in his hands and kisses her lips as the violins burble and the sunset dies like a smear of raspberry jam on the cyclorama.

Skeets Kalbfleischer is also a film star of sorts. A file composed of ancient newsreels, newspaper clippings, and hospital training films is stored in the memory bank under the general classification Medicine, subheading Surgery. Skeets has programmed his file several times, out of the same morbid curiosity which once caused men to peek under their own bandages.

The film is a history of mankind's first successful cerebrectomy. It tells the story of a twelve-year-old boy named Denton Kalbfleischer, who was returning home with his parents to Joliet, Illinois, from a Christmas skiing vacation in Vail, Colorado. While circling O'Hare Field in a holding pattern prior to landing, his jetliner was apparently hit by lightning. The result was, at that time, the worst air disaster in aviation history. Over five hundred people were killed, more than half of them on the ground, as bits of molten 747 rained down on East Cicero like a meteor shower. And when, amidst the din of sirens, a fireman found Skeets' broken body heaped on a curbside pile of rubble, it was assumed he was a neighborhood boy, injured by falling debris. Only many hours later, during a routine check of the passenger lists, was his correct identity discovered.

The newspapers, of course, had a field day. Banner headlines proclaimed a XMAS MIRACLE and a swarm of reporters descended like encircling vultures on the Kalbfleischers' Joliet home to interview the maid, the neighbors, the postman, Skeets' sixth-grade teacher, anyone at all with even the vaguest connection to "that courageous, freckle-faced kid fighting for his life on the fifth floor of the Cook County Hospital." Skeets' parents, Dr. and Mrs. Harold Kalbfleischer, were killed in the crash, but home movies the family took the summer before at Narragansett, Rhode Island, were broadcast in color on all the major television networks. Skeets and his dad playing catch on the beach.

Newsreel cameramen stalked the corridors of the hospital, ambushing unwary doctors for filmed firsthand reports and occasionally sneaking past the security guards for a chance at valuable footage of poor Skeets, so savagely mangled that his body could not tolerate the pressure of an ordinary hospital bed, floating like a mummified Hindu levitation artist on a cushion of compressed air. Although, for the benefit of the press, the hospital staff remained cheerfully optimistic, in private Skeets' doctors held out little hope for recovery. Virtually every major bone was fractured, arms and legs shattered, the spinal vertebrae crushed and disconnected like a broken string of beads; all the internal organs ruptured and hemorrhaging; rib fragments punctured both lungs—even considering the recent advances in the field of organ transplants, surgical teams across the nation agreed the case was hopeless. In order to save Skeets they would have to rebuild him from scratch.

A Hollywood film, late in the second reel, would call in a handsome young specialist for delicate, last-minute surgery; happy ending: Skeets lives to play football again and the successful surgeon gets the bosomy blond night nurse with the heart of gold. Reality is more prosaic. The memory-file program cuts to an old videotape of the medical laboratory at the Space Center in Houston, Texas, where the mechanical narrator introduces a NASA engineer, Dr. Frank E. Sayre, Jr. Dr. Sayre has thinning hair, combed straight back, and wears bifocals. For the past five years he has been engaged in special research dealing with the problem of space environment. It is Dr. Sayre's contention that man's body is a liability on a space mission. It must be supplied with oxygen, shielded from extreme temperature variation and radioactivity, provided with food, and let's not forget the nasty business of waste removal. All this requires complex weighty equipment.

"Weight is a critical factor in the success of these missions," Dr. Sayre says, nervously toying with his slide-rule tieclasp. "Now it always seemed to me that going to all this expense and trouble to accommodate the human body on a space flight was putting the cart before the horse, if you understand my meaning." Dr. Sayre clears his throat and continues in a soft sugarcured Tidelands accent. "The only essential part of a man, the part that can't be duplicated mechanically on a spacecraft, is his brain. The rest is simply excess baggage. I approached the problem from the point of view of an engineer. Wouldn't it be wonderful if we could find some way to integrate a man's brain with the control system of a space vehicle and leave all that other junk at home in the deep freeze? It would make long-range manned space probes—something on the order of a trip to Pluto, say—feasible right now, today, instead of in a hundred years or so as is currently predicted."

The narration resumes at this point to explain how Dr. Sayre was inspired by the work of a team of Russian scientists who successfully grafted the head of one dog onto the body of another. Using similar surgical techniques, Dr. Sayre was busy for the next few years scooping the brains out of a zooful of rhesus monkeys. The primitive equipment he used grew ever more refined as his government research grants increased and by the time the film was made he had amassed over half a million dollars' worth in the corner of his lab. Although this jumble of tubing and circuitry looks quite haphazard and comical when compared with the sleek efficient Depositories into which it evolved, the essential mechanism remains the same. In Dr. Sayre's day it resembled nothing more than a pet shop fishtank. He is shown in the film posing with a big smile beside this device. Inside, floating in the electrolyte solution, is something that looks like a pinkish-gray jellyfish. This is the brain of George, a nine-year-old orangutan, which, according to the encephalograph, was still alive sixteen months after Dr. Sayre wheeled his great orange-haired body to the incinerator.

A phone call from a colleague in Chicago brought the case of Denton Kalbfleischer to Dr. Sayre's attention. The boy was very near death and, as there seemed to be no living relatives around to object, perhaps the hospital staff might be willing to attempt a radical experiment. Negotiations were conducted and that same evening Dr. Sayre and all his apparatus were on board a northbound plane. Inside of twenty-four hours, George had a roommate in the fishtank.

The newspapers were told that Skeets had died and the reporters were all there when his body was buried in the family plot. It was a closed-coffin funeral. The official press release mentioned a Scout uniform with merit badges and a beloved fielder's mitt under the pale folded hands, but these were only lies designed to satisfy a sentimental public. After the operation, the body was wrapped in a black plastic bag and sent to its final rest with the tracheotomy tubes still in place and the skull open like an empty porcelain soup tureen.

A color film of the operation was secretly placed in the

hospital archives for the elucidation of future surgeons. Shots of the shaved scalp being peeled forward like a bathing cap and of surgical saws neatly carving through the cranium are especially vivid, but unfortunately a section of the print was damaged at the point where a vacuum pump lifts the brain intact, the enveloping meninges untorn. Cuts from other, later operations had to be spliced into the memory-file. Because a more sophisticated technique was then employed, certain concessions were made and the narrator politely apologizes to the viewer for the slight lapse in chronological accuracy.

After the operation, Skeets' brain remained incognito for almost two years in Dr. Sayre's Houston laboratory, a lump of gray matter distinguishable from the others in the tank only by the added number of wrinkles on its convoluted surface. NASA was no longer interested in the experiment once federal funds were cut back in an election year Congressional economy drive, and Dr. Sayre kept the brains around more or less as pets. Skeets would have been doomed to this limbo forever if an overanxious hunter hadn't mistaken the balding scientist for a mule deer while he was out bird watching early one fine fall morning. After the funeral, his widow came across an unpublished notebook among the papers on his desk. It was a day-to-day record of Skeets' progress following the operation. Mrs. Sayre instinctively knew this was the instrument that not only would save her late husband's name from obscurity, but handsomely endow his meager estate as well.

When the news broke, as a cover story in *Life,* the ancient periodical photo magazine, public reaction was immediate. Panels of clergymen convened to discuss the ethics of such operations. The Bar Association appointed a special commission to study the legal rights of cerebromorphs. The AMA got in on the action by condemning unauthorized experimentation on hospital patients. Across the country there were hundreds of volunteers for cerebrectomy. Many of these individuals were already signed up to have their bodies frozen in liquid nitrogen after death. Now they wanted to place all bets on a sure thing. Enterprising morticians modified their facilities and advertised what were soon to become the world's first Depositories.

As for Skeets, Mrs. Sayre turned down a very generous offer from a traveling circus and donated him to Johns Hopkins, her husband's alma mater. There he spent the next twenty-five years as a curiosity, a prize specimen gathering dust in a graduate school laboratory, until advancing technology at last provided the elaborate mechanism that put him once again in touch with the outside world. The historic moment when the Bell Laboratory technicians hooked Skeets up to Dr. deHartzman's ingenious neural communicator was televised internationally and portions of the preserved videotape provide a fine ending for the memory-file presentation.

In keeping with the occasion, the president of the university prepared a statement clearly intended to live forever: "Mankind proudly welcomes back the intrepid voyager into the unknown." But history is not so easily juggled with and it is Skeets' answer that is remembered, not the president's eloquent words. There was a crackle of static on the loudspeaker system as the boy got used to his new computerized electric vocal cords and then, in a smooth machined monotone, he asked, "What time is breakfast?"

And so ends memory-file number M109-36S. It documents the world's first cerebrectomy in an entertaining, yet educational, manner, but omits the most significant part of Skeets Kalbfleischer's incredible story. There is no mention of the twenty-five years Skeets spent alone in darkness. Not one word to describe the explosive holocaust in which his dreams were born; the instant of absolute terror when the jetliner disintegrated in a ball of flame and he was torn loose from his fastened seatbelt; his clothing and hair, even the comic book he was reading, ignited by the blast that sent him tumbling down through five miles of open sky like a shooting star. It was the beginning of a nightmare a quarter century long.

Obu Itubi is a bee, or almost anyway, for the memory-file is one of a recent series which includes a separate track for each of the senses. Itubi can smell the heat and the sweet dusty pollen; he can feel the jostling of his busy neighbors, the furred armor of their pulsing abdomens. The drone of thousands of transparent wings is programmed into his auditory nerves. His is a bee's-eye view of the hive: the perfect geometric succession of hexagonal cells, the interlinked pattern of the comb, membranous waxen walls. To his sculptor's sensibility it seems pure poetry in the use of materials—nature's harmony, the ultimate technology. Here is real elegance in engineering, a refinement sadly lacking in this age of contemplation. Moreover, the whole unit is organic. Itubi is awed.

As the file progresses, Itubi happily participates in the worker's directional waggle-dance. He gathers pollen, produces honey and joins with thousands of others in the heat of midday to fan his wings and keep the delicate wax structures from melting. He is proud of his six clinging legs, the sensitive jointed antennae, the potent stinger. He feels lost and empty when the file comes to an end and he is no longer a bee.

And yet, transmission fade-out is something Itubi has always enjoyed. First there is the image (in this case, the busy swarm of *Apis mellifera*) flooding his consciousness like sunlight and then, with only the briefest command from the telescript console, it's gone, the whole universe of thought receding into a tiny pinpoint in the frontal lobe. It hovers for a moment, a candle flame in the eternal night, very serene and distant. The final flickering seems almost an invitation: follow me, follow me. . . . Itubi wonders how many men have lingered in the evening at the edge of a lonely marsh to watch the flitting light of the will-o'-the-wisp? At such times liberation seems almost possible. But at the very instant of the soul's release, the candle is snuffed and you are left alone in the dark.

Vera Mitlovic is deep in a celluloid dreamland: the fashion designer back at her drawing-board, a faraway look in her violet eyes as the old film drowns in a climactic violin whirlpool. "All lost," the disembodied actress muses, consulting the Index for the number of yet another film. Not any film this time—for it is usually Vera's habit to choose her entertainment by whim and random selection—but her very first, made in Vienna when she was six. The great Klimpt was directing, and although she had only a bit part, the magnificent ballroom scenes never fail to lift her spirits and she can think of no more effective antidote for melancholy than her own brief appearance in pigtails and pinafore.

She finds the correct code number for *The Golden Epoch* and activates the telescript console. To Vera, this device is one of the few gay toys in her spiritless mechanical universe. Think of a number and, like rubbing a magic lantern, within seconds a memory-file materializes. When her wish doesn't come true, Vera is puzzled. Can there have been a breakdown in the System? She repeats the number, pausing between each digit so there will be no mistake. Again, nothing happens.

This is alarming. The Depository System functions automatically, although breakdowns are not unknown. Precise emergency procedures and periodic drills ensure the alertness of the residents. Vera was at the movies during drill and now finds she is helpless in the face of actual crisis.

The clear musical clarion of a deHartzman Communicator is as reassuring as the nick-of-time cavalry bugle call when the wagon train is surrounded by rampaging Sioux. A silent wind sweeps the prairie.

ATTENTION . . . ATTENTION . . .

The mood shifts. The mechanical voice has the moronic robot enthusiasm of an AM radio disk jockey from another age.

CENTER CONTROL IS TEMPORARILY INTERRUPTING YOUR THOUGHTS TO COMMUNICATE AN AWARENESS REMINDER FROM THE AUDITING COMMISSION. . . . STAND BY . . .

B-0486 . . . IT HAS NOW BEEN THREE DAYS SINCE YOU LAST PARTICIPATED IN THE MORNING MEDITATION EXERCISE OR FILED AN AUDITING REPORT. THIS IS A VIOLATION OF SECTIONS A15, A16, AND C9 OF REGULATION NUMBER 35-095. IN ACCORDANCE WITH THE MANDATE OF CENTER CONTROL, WE ARE DISCONNECTING YOUR MEMORY-BANK HOOKUP UNTIL SUCH TIME AS YOU ARE WILLING TO FULFILL THE OBLIGATIONS OF YOUR CATEGORY. BE AWARE OF YOUR DUTIES.

END TRANSMISSION.

Vera Mitlovic is furious. Another move in the game, the

obvious machine-tooled move. She remembers tick-tack-toe. Twentieth-century scientists taught their primitive Univacs to play this kindergarten game years before they were able to program complex chess gambits. And how those old machines loved it! Vacuum tubes aglow, rectifiers humming, they paraded their invincible Xs out across the graph, winning all encounters if given the first move, tying the rest. It pleases Vera to think of the proud Univac, defeating the best scientific minds of the age at a child's game, victorious until the mathematicians pulled the plug and went home for lunch.

But this time the plug has been pulled on Vera. She is tempted to try the telescript console one more time but resists, not wanting to give those transistorized swine in the Auditing Commission the pleasure of knowing her desperation. Vera still has her fierce pride. She didn't leave that on the operating table.

Skeets Kalbfleischer's Auditor is a cerebromorph of some celebrity, a pioneer astronaut, the surviving member of the melancholy Aldebaran Expedition and the only resident of Level II born in the twentieth century.

Philip Quarrels was flying a carrier-based F4 Phantom over the Mekong Delta at the time of the great Chicago disaster. The name Denton Kalbfleischer meant nothing to him; his interest in the accident was purely aeronautical. When

Skeets' brain made the cover of *Life* two years later, Quarrels was training for a future Apollo shot and read the article only because a former NASA member had been involved. Cerebrectomy was for crackpots, not the Space Program.

The Space Program was Philip Quarrels' life work. He was lunar module pilot on the final Apollo flight. Later he worked on the space-platform project and, because he was unmarried, Quarrels was chosen as the first long-term skipper on the U.S. Orbital Station *Endeavor.* He spent the next fifteen years in space, shuttling between platform assignments and desk jobs in the moon base at Clavius.

Because he was largely indifferent to happenings on earth, Quarrels knew nothing of the worldwide public indifference to the Mars landing of 1985. People were bored with television coverage of the moon and pictures from yet another dead planet didn't satisfy. Oceanography had replaced ecology as a trendsetter; films of undersea exploration earned an average twenty percentage points higher in the ratings than any broadcast from space. The following year, when the Venus Expedition was lost, Congress voted to cut the space budget in half.

In 1990, the year Philip Quarrels was due to retire, Skeets Kalbfleischer made the headlines for a second time when Dr. Tibor deHartzman perfected the first neural communicator. NASA soon took another look at the work of Frank E. Sayre, Jr. A daring new mission to the Aldebaran binary system was announced. The voyage would take three hundred years, round trip. Cerebromorphs would compose the crew. The call went out for volunteers, men with long space experience and without families. Age was no handicap. Even retired astronauts were encouraged to apply. Eventually a crew of five was selected. Captain Philip Quarrels was named Executive Officer.

A twentieth-century astronaut is a hero Skeets Kalbfleischer can admire and he is very impressed with his Auditor. Skeets means a lot to Quarrels as well. Fifty years of hard work. Each Auditor carries a caseload of ten lower-level residents and is in turn audited by a resident of the level above. Elevation comes with Awareness and Understanding. One Auditor audits another; reports are made to the Commission; Center Control sets the standards.

Quarrels' career in the navy has accustomed him to moving through the ranks. He is anxious for elevation, which he still unconsciously refers to as promotion. His Auditor is working hard on the problem. By bringing others to Understanding, one's own Awareness grows.

Skeets Kalbfleischer prepares an auditing report. He replays the memo file of his dream twice, editing those portions which appear to have no significance. As much as he enjoys the long blimp ride with a gondola full of starlets or his own erotic version of *Sleeping Beauty*, where he awakens the princess with something more emphatic than a kiss, he erases these reveries from the file without hesitation. Skeets is only interested in his nightmares.

This particular nocturnal horror is nothing new. Skeets has suffered through it many times in the past, but because of its brevity he has never before attempted an analysis for the Auditing Commission. Not that it is very difficult to trace the origins of the dream; even after a fifty-year lapse, Skeets is able to list the memory-files which are the source material for his terror.

He viewed them originally during his studies of Eastern art. The first he programmed by mistake, thinking he was to see a Cambodian temple dance. Its title, "Monkey-Moon Ceremony," was misleading. The file actually deals with a ceremonial banquet peculiar to the highland regions of Laos and Cambodia. For the first course, a smooth stone table, several inches thick, with a perfect round aperture cut through the center, is brought into the banquet hall. The guests seat themselves, arranging their robes and bowing with mannered formality. Soon a bronze gong sounds and the servants bring a live monkey, limbs trussed in an attitude of prayer. The monkey is placed under the stone table with the top of his head protruding through the opening in the center. The servants complete their arrangements, providing each guest with a long silver spoon. When all is ready, the host gives a curt nod and his chief retainer unsheathes a short gleaming double-edged sword and, leaning forward, slices off the top of the monkey's skull as easily as he would uncap a soft-boiled egg. A chattering gibberish continues underneath the table as the dinner guests, each in his turn, sample the monkey's brain. There is just enough for everyone to have a taste. Happy smiles all around attest to the excellence of the dish. The host claps his hands and calls loudly for the soup.

The second file Skeets programmed deliberately, after searching through the Index for the correct code key, his curiosity inflamed. He found a Chinese variation of the same culinary eccentricity. A different place-setting is used: along with each set of chopsticks, a small golden mallet is provided. The monkey is brought to the table confined in a cage and passes among the guests, who reach between the bars and give the cowering animal a discreet tap with the mallet. The cage is circulated many times and, as the blows are never strong enough to stun, the monkey continues to voice his complaints in a high-pitched wail which greatly amuses the worthy Oriental gentlemen.

At last it is over. The dazed monkey is removed from the cage, a sharp knife skins away his scalp, and the shattered skull is picked apart piece by piece in a manner which reminds Skeets of the way he used to deal with hard-boiled eggs.

It is this similarity to eating eggs that bothers Skeets. He remembers his mother serving them to him at breakfast, standing upright in little painted cups. He dipped fingers of buttered toast into the yolk and ate the whites with his baby spoon. When he finished, the hollow shell looked clean and bleached, like a skull. He mentions this on the auditing report as a prelude to his dream.

The dream itself is quite simple. Skeets is looking through the scanner. He sees an Amco-pak maintenance van approaching down the aisle, silently gliding past the anonymous pale-blue façade of the Depository. The machine stops in front of his deposit drawer and removes his cranial container without a word. Somehow, Skeets is able to watch through the scanner as the Amco-pak carries him out of the Sector into a region which is totally unfamiliar.

A set of stainless-steel doors slide open and Skeets is brought into a large chamber and set on a feast table in front of twelve jolly diners, all of whom look like Humpty Dumpty. They are talking Chinese! The Amco-pak opens the lid of the cranial container and, without further ceremony, the bizarre Mother Goose figures proceed to dip slices of buttered toast into poor Skeets' frontal lobe. "Yum-yum," they cry, in Nanking dialect. Skeets watches it all until there is nothing left of him but a few stray crumbs of gray matter floating on the oily surface of the electrolyte solution. He has had this dream at least once a week for the last fifty years.

2. Pupa

THE AISLES ARE QUIET. Only the most determined residents still tune to their scanners, waiting patiently for something to happen. It is rumored that certain of the Advanced Sectors use neither scanners nor communicators (blinded by their own *satori*, as the saying goes). In the subdistrict such total isolation would be unthinkable. Most residents are satisfied with the empty aisles. They would be lost without the squat lead-covered power units and accompanying trio of deHartzman Communicators, radar domes aglow and multifrequency channel finders blinking like beacons.

In Aisle B, Obu Itubi consults the memory-file Index, looking for a recent program on spiders. He is interested in the dynamics of web construction and anticipates the pleasures of spinning silk and weaving intricate patterns. The warning tone of a deHartzman Communicator interrupts his quiet study.

ATTENTION . . . THERE IS A TOP-PRIORITY IN-COMING
COMMUNICATION ORIGINATING FROM CENTER CONTROL . . .
ALL CIRCUITS WILL OPEN AUTOMATICALLY IN TEN SECONDS
. . . STAND BY . . .

Itubi thinks of herald trumpets; ten seconds for proper
spiritual attitudes, the attentive acolyte awaits the go-ahead
signal.

BEEP . . .

Hello.

GOOD MORNING, B-0489, WE TRUST THAT YOU SPENT A
PEACEFUL NIGHT AND HAVE ALL YOUR THOUGHTS IN HAR-
MONY.

Everything is as I would wish it.

GOOD. WE ARE COMMUNICATING WITH YOU, B-0489, TO
ANNOUNCE THAT YOUR PRESENT AUDITOR HAS BEEN ELE-
VATED TO 64 DEGREES OF UNDERSTANDING AND TRANS-
FERRED TO LEVEL III. WE ARE SURE YOU WILL CELEBRATE HIS
SUCCESS JOYFULLY.

The Wise Man learns the Way by following the path of
those who have gone before.

YES, BUT THE WISE MAN MUST ALSO REMEMBER THAT
THERE EXISTS FOR HIM BUT ONE PATH WHICH IS TRUE.
ADMIRATION FOR OTHERS NEVER MISLEADS THE WISE MAN
INTO TAKING A WRONG TURN. B-0489, YOU HAVE BEEN
ASSIGNED A NEW AUDITOR. HE HAS SPENT SEVERAL WEEKS
STUDYING YOUR FILES, AND RATHER THAN WASTE TIME

WITH FURTHER FORMALITIES LET US CONNECT YOU WITH
HIM IMMEDIATELY.

*All greetings, B-0489, before we begin, are there any ques-
tions you would like to ask?*

It is the fool who speaks; the Wise Man listens.

*Very true, B-0489, so if you'll listen now, I'll simplify the
introductions. My files are on record in the memory bank,
code key Y41-AK9(397-00-55). I invite your investigation of
them at any time. That should satisfy all social obligations.*

Yes.

*Then let's get down to business. If it agrees with you,
we'll maintain the same auditing schedule you had in the
past. My predecessor made a practice of infrequent communication—*

To permit independent study and encourage—

*We shall abandon that practice. The auditing schedule
will be followed exactly. Sessions begin promptly. Any time
lapse will result in additional assignments. Do you understand?*

Yes.

*Good. Before we end transmission, I'd like to clear up a
few points with you. First, I notice you've been programming memory-bank files almost at random. There is no
logic to your selections. You don't seem to follow any regular pattern of study. Six months ago you spent your time listening to music; recently you only screen files dealing with
insect behavior. Is there a reason for this?*

The Wise Man strives to keep an open mind, and—

You can save the doubletalk! I don't care to hear your clever explanations. I want you to know that further erratic behavior will not be tolerated. The memory bank is not a frivolous plaything designed for your personal amusement. You forget, B-0489, you're no longer a famous artist. All that is gone forever. You are simply a resident cerebromorph on file in the lowest level of the Depository System. Learn to function within the System. One of the obligations of your category is to obey all social regulations faithfully. One cannot possibly hope to shed the illusions of identity without first accepting the responsibility of society.

Thank you for reminding me. The Voyager into the Unknown frequently loses his way.

B-0489, I compliment you on your flattery. It undoubtedly impresses Center Control and puts you in good favor with the authorities. But let me remind you that I am familiar with your files. So, don't waste the honeyed words. Our first appointment is scheduled for tomorrow at 0019. I trust that will give you sufficient time to get your thoughts in order. Remember to be prompt.

End transmission.

CLICK.

Vera Mitlovic hates being alone. Even as a young girl many centuries ago, she detested aimless walks in the rain, or afternoons in quiet museums, or any of the other solitary pleasures to which romantic youth is traditionally disposed. She craved a continual audience. Surrounded by constant admirers, Vera was splendid, she dazzled and charmed; without her makeup, alone, she felt lost and afraid, like a confused chameleon unable to revert to its original hue. She faced a stranger in the wardrobe mirror, the eyes that stared back provided no clue, they were bright with the sham glitter of costume jewelry.

And so Vera played various roles, on camera and off, before a succession of accidental friends, casual lovers, and supernumerary husbands. She took her cues from the moment. As a young star in Prague, she was a properly zealous socialist artist, bright, literate and opinionated. She became an instant patriot the night of the Cannes Film Festival when she rose in her seat to denounce the Russian intervention and brought tears to the eyes of everyone present, including the French producer who, a half hour earlier, had offered her a lucrative five-year contract if she would defect. For ten years the reigning sex queen on the Continent, she was photographed frequently wearing only a pastel mink, owned a different color Rolls for each day of the week, and when asked about diamonds said that she preferred the big ones, naturally.

While in her forties, her voice lowered by an octave, she abandoned the films for a stage career, played Medea at Epidaurus and Lady Macbeth at Stratford, became the darling of the homosexual set, and attempted suicide on two occasions, meeting with only moderate success. By the time her hair turned white, she was ensconced in international society. At fifty-five she married a doddering Italian nobleman who responded to her enduring sexual ferocity with an abrupt coronary before the honeymoon was six days old.

Vera's finest role was that of the majestic widow. She was every inch the quattrocento duchess. The pawnshop escutcheon of the Medici surmounted the entrance to her palazzo overlooking the Arno. She kept a villa in Fiesole to house her collection of exotic animals and startled the complacent Florentines by parading under the arcade along the Piazza della Repubblica with two bewigged blacks holding her brocade train, a baboon straining on one golden leash, an ocelot on another, and her scandalous retinue chattering at her elbow in a variety of tongues.

As Vera grew older her fear of being alone developed into a mania. Her house overflowed with guests. The young man of the moment was always there to turn down the sheets at night. Like the Sun King, she employed special servants to assist her onto a fur-lined toilet seat. Secretaries arranged her day to prevent any chance of privacy. Death, of course, remained the ultimate solitude, and the bulk of the ducal fortune was expended to forestall that eventuality. There were periodic trips to Switzerland for rejuvenating monkey-gland injections. Cosmeticians ironed away wrinkles, inserted silicone into sagging breasts, and tucked a series of chins up somewhere behind her ears. When one heart failed a team of surgeons rushed in to replace it with another. Collapsed veins were reinforced with plastic tubing. A gangrenous hand was removed and a mechanical silver replica from Van Cleef and Arpels set a fashion trend which started hundreds of women throughout the world clamoring for amputation.

When the second millennium was thirty years old, Vera celebrated her one-hundredth birthday, a plumber's miracle of transplanted organs and artificial limbs. She delighted her guests by eating a piece of cake and drinking three glasses of champagne. For fifteen years Vera was fed intravenously, after advanced cancer necessitated the removal of her entire intestinal tract. Later surgeons inserted a highly serviceable latex receptacle that emptied through a valve in her navel and was flushed clean each month with liquid detergent. "Now I can eat and never get fat," she laughingly told her partner as the orchestra began another tango. Dancing was no problem for Vera. Her arthritic outmoded joints had long since been supplanted by efficient self-lubricating nylon hinges. She was limber as a teenager.

It seemed to Vera that she would live forever; the party would go on without end. Certainly she was durable enough. Her lungs were still sound, and even if they gave out an ingenious battery-powered oxygenator was soon to be mass produced by the same South African firm that successfully marketed the first portable mechanical kidney. It was reassuring to know there was no shortage of replacement parts.

Also, luck seemed to be on Vera's side. When the Thirty-minute Thermonuclear War of 2066 atomized every major city in North America and Asia and girdled the earth with radioactive clouds that reduced the populations of Europe and the Near East by two-thirds, Vera was safely in Santiago de Chile on a round-the-world tour. Even the financial chaos that followed left her unscathed. Vera's money was in South American and African holdings and she watched her fortune triple as those continents rose to world dominance in the final decades of the twenty-first century.

In the long run, Vera felt the war had done a lot of good. Certainly Europe seemed much nicer now that it wasn't so crowded; no more camera-ladened Americans jammed the streets. And the way the old buildings glowed in the dark was really romantic. The rash of two-headed babies was unfortunate, but the United Nations Euthanasia Corps (UNEC) soon eliminated the problem and the possibility of bearing monsters was a good incentive for population control. All in all, the world was much improved, a fine place in which to live forever.

But Vera's plans for eternal life were upset one morning when her doctor made his weekly medical report. Vera's health was fine. Her body could be maintained mechanically for an indefinite time. The trouble was, in spite of everything, the old woman was fast approaching senility. It seemed a shame, for certain recent advances in geriatric endocrinology would eventually eliminate the problem. But treatment had to be started by the age of 100. If only she were fifty years younger. A real pity, to watch the mind deteriorate. Of course, there was an alternative, a bit drastic perhaps, but— "Anything," Vera pleaded. The doctor recommended cerebrectomy.

Deep within the complexity of Center Control, a labyrinth of microcircuits, conductors, directional transmitters, relay switches, and transistors extending for almost a square mile at the heart of the Depository System, a special series of computer banks (ordinarily assigned to the regulation of an entire subdistrict) is considering the problem of Skeets Kalbfleischer. Because of his symbolic importance, it is intolerable that Skeets still resides on the lowest level of the System. Recent analysis shows that the Elevation of mankind's original cerebromorph will have profound spiritual results. The Ascension of Jesus Christ and the Enlightenment of Gautama Siddhartha are mentioned as comparable transcendental events.

Skeets is not uncooperative. For two hundred and seventy years he has diligently followed every study program outlined for him by Center Control. He faithfully participates in the meditation exercise each morning. He hasn't filed a late auditing report in nearly a century. But, in spite of this exemplary behavior, Skeets still registers close to 100 on the Ego Scale each time a diagnosis is made. Deep in his subconscious, Skeets prefers riding the range and packing a six-gun to fasting, navel contemplation, and walking on water. As far as he is concerned, one man's *karma* is another man's *dharma*.

Obu Itubi remembers the bee: a million identical larvae pupating within the privacy of their waxen cells—one million identical dreams. All share a common destiny, all but a dozen or so selected at random by the workers in charge of the hatchery cells. These fortunate few are fortified with an infusion of Royal Jelly, an extract that transforms any ordinary larva into a Queen. A drop is all it takes. Instant royalty. And the new Queen is wise in the ways of monarchy from the moment of her birth. Her first official act is political assassination. Even before her wings have dried, the newly hatched Queen seeks out the cells of potential rivals and quickly stings them to death while they drift in embryonic sleep.

A sweet thought: Obu Itubi would like to be so chosen. He imagines an Amco-pak Mark X adding some magic elixir to the electrolyte solution in his cranial container and emerging from the Depository a king, all-powerful and absolute. He would roam the aisles until he found the deposit drawer containing his new Auditor. Let the bastard enjoy his spiritual superiority while he has the chance, Itubi thinks. My triumph will be complete when I puncture the sanctity of his computerized dreams and skewer him like a shish kebab on the tip of my envenomed blade. A fitting final lesson in the Illusion of Identity.

A Unistat Magnetic Calculator, series 3000, assigned to the Census Division of Center Control, has discovered an error so incredible that the machine suspects a short circuit and turns itself in for an overhaul and parts checkup. But Maintenance and Repair can find nothing amiss and a doublecheck by the Census Division verifies the Unistat's findings: a resident of Level I (the lowest in the System) has been misfiled.

For a time it seems this alarming discovery will necessitate a review of the entire filing system. Any calculator error is considered inexcusable by Center Control and an order consigning the Unistat Series 3000 to the junkheap is immediately issued. The controversial series 4000A, which has languished on the drawing boards for seventy-five years, is hurried into production.

The indirect cause of all this turmoil is Skeets Kalbfleischer. In his Auditor's opinion, Skeets' failure to advance spiritually is the result of being trapped in Eternal adolescence. His fantasies are purely masturbatory. His phobias the result of puberty. In short, the boy needs to get laid.

Skeets, of course, has already experienced orgasm. It can be induced electronically in the cranial container at the flip of a switch. Special electrodes are directly wired to the appropriate nerve endings. A resident only has to dial the corresponding code key on his telescript console. Technology has improved upon nature; a biological orgasm lasts a few seconds; the electronic version continues until the current is switched off.

Acting on the advice of Philip Quarrels, Skeets endures a climax lasting almost three days. Shock treatment to satisfy the voracious sexual demands of his adolescent mind. The experiment is a failure. Skeets enjoys the pornographic memory-files, but, all in all, it is a run-of-the-mill wet dream. Spontaneity and imagination are preferable to long-distance mileage.

But the Auditing Commission is undaunted. Mere sensation obviously isn't the answer. What the boy needs is actual experience, his own private love affair. An easy matter to arrange. A two-party memory-merge requires only the most basic rewiring, nothing like the multiple hookups needed for more sophisticated group experience. The only problem is locating the correct partner. The Census Division is asked to find a resident female, born in the middle of the twentieth century, who had sexual relations with a twelve-year-old boy.

The twentieth century has the lowest population in the Depository System and it takes a Unistat 3000 less than an hour to run through all the female files. It comes up with the numbers of nearly fifty women who had amused themselves with long-dead delivery boys. Three are ex–school teachers who centuries before had seduced precocious students in coat rooms and under desks. None of these will do. They had all been middle-aged (some nearly sixty) when they developed a taste for prepubescence and it is feared the age discrepancy might prove too traumatic for Skeets. In order to satisfy the Auditors, the female merge-partner has to be nearly the same age as the boy: an eager virgin with undeveloped breasts and slim athletic hips, seasoned by nothing stronger than puppy-love.

The Unistat 3000 tries again and draws a blank. The Census Division recommends an early twenty-first-century female; increased Depository population allows for a wider choice and, owing to the liberal mores of the age, a twelve-year-old without sexual experience is a rarity. Again, the Auditors say no. The time difference is too great; memories are liable to be disparate and the resulting merge would seem more like fantasy than reality. What Skeets needs is a strong dose of reality.

The Auditing Commission is insistent. Top priority must be given the Kalbfleischer affair. Center Control is firmly behind the project and the methodical examination of all possible channels officially encouraged. It is suggested to the Deltron Unistat Coordinator (a machine whose singular lack of

humor and fanatic concern for detail make it the most efficient Director of Census in over a century) that a cross-refer-
ence check with the files of other divisions might prove
productive. The Unistat goes to work immediately and five
hours later, while running through a routine batch of old
auditing reports, a Series 3000 makes the astonishing discovery. Sometime late in the twenty-second century, when the
last private depositories were incorporated, the brain of a mid-
twentieth-century cinema actress was inadvertently misfiled.

To throw the Auditing Commission off track, in case they
should be monitoring his telescript console, Obu Itubi submits a study plan along with his new batch of memory-file
requests. The plan includes an elaborate apology for his
unfortunate philanthropy together with a resolution to over-
come a basic prejudice toward machines. As part of his program for achieving tolerance and understanding, Itubi
requests the complete plans and wiring diagrams for all of
the Amco-pak series above Mark V. If he can learn to appreciate the complexities of even a simple machine like the
Amco-pak, Itubi is certain it won't be long before he is filled
with admiration for his cybernetic superiors.

Memory-merge. The term has always disgusted Vera Mitlovic. There is something repulsive about the blend of
mechanics and sentiment. Vera remembers certain drooling

lovers (handfuls of ashes in lonesome marble urns), impossible romantics who interpreted a few minutes of pleasant friction and the discharge of a tablespoon of semen as something cosmic, a union of souls. How had she ever endured such fools? In her prime Vera had been an accomplished sexual athlete and if she screamed a bit during orgasm it wasn't in celebration of the primordial pagan pieties. She paid no homage to the dark gods of the blood. What Vera craved was technique and innovation. She much preferred the skillful application of whip and harness to the attentions of any man who felt his penis was an extension of the Infinite. In fact, of all the young gallants who showed up at her dressing room with expensive bouquets and elegant flattery, the one she remembers best is a wall-eyed count who lashed her naked breasts with his gift offering of long-stemmed roses.

So if Vera receives the news of her impending memory-merge with something less than elation, it is because she is satisfied with the past as she lived it. What need has she for a metaphysical love affair? Her own recollections are sufficiently erotic (the stinging kiss of the thorns, her second husband's playful habit of sharing her with his Great Dane), and if she desires immediate satisfaction, she can dial for an orgasm at any time, night or day.

Skeets Kalbfleischer prepares for his first date. Centuries before, when he still had hair to comb and teeth to brush, he

would have forestalled his nervousness in front of the bath-
room mirror, plastering his cowlick down with Vaseline and
water, polishing his smile and mentholating his breath.
There would have been difficult Windsor knots to be tied
and retied until the ends of the unfamiliar four-in-hand hung
exactly even; shoes would have to be flawlessly shined; fingernails cleaned; pants pressed—a million trivial details to
make the time go faster. But, alone in the eternity of his cranial container, Skeets is without armpits to deodorize or
acne to conceal. He is trapped, like the Titans in Tartarus, in
a world where time has ceased to exist.

The blueprints for the Amco-pak series come through without difficulty. Itubi is pleased. The Auditing Commission
must be relishing his contrition. Another soul saved. Score
another point for technology. Somewhere an unknown calculator adds his name to the list, a cipher among ciphers. Itubi
is unconcerned. Let the Auditors enjoy their false triumph;
what he wants are the blueprints.
   They are exact detailed plans, reproduced three-dimension-
ally on the memory-file. The diagrams and scale drawings
seem almost to float in Itubi's consciousness, like models
spun from fine glowing wire, a cobweb designed by an electri-
cal engineer. Itubi is able to view the plans in the round; he
can study them from any angle, from above, along the sides,
underneath. His early training as a machinist (a part of his

boyhood he had always resented) now does him yeoman's service. The complexities of the Amco-pak are easily unraveled. In less than an hour, Itubi has memorized the plans.

Kalbfleischer? Kalbfleischer? What sort of name is that? Vera Mitlovic is positive it sounds Jewish. A rich American Jew. They were trying to humiliate her. Once before, advised by her Auditor, she underwent not a merge, but a simple memory transfer. It was felt that maternity would be a beneficial experience for Vera (all of her marriages and affairs were barren) and so she experienced prerecorded childbirth. Vera was in labor for over thirty hours, the delivery a nightmare of forceps and clamps. As instruments of torture, not even the racks and wheels of the Inquisition could rival that hideous table with its fiendish straps and stirrups. Now they add insult to injury by preparing this merge with a Jew. Somehow Vera will persevere. She's lived through worse. It might even prove a diverting novelty, like a Chinese or a black. Certainly, it will be better than being alone.

Obu Itubi is ready at last. The moment for action has come. Without ending his original transmission, he simultaneously submits three random memory-bank requests. The warning light blinks on and off. Itubi ignores it and activates his communicator antenna. The light is blinking faster now. Itubi opens all circuits. The Memo Center clicks on, a distant humming in his guts. Gyros spinning, feedback eliminator up to full, magnetic relay-transfer switch to the on position, photon oscillator near the danger point. The warning light goes berserk as all systems function and Itubi is alive, alive. . . .

Like a prizefight manager at ringside, Auditor Philip Quarrels is hurriedly giving Skeets last-minute advice. He warns the boy of the ephemeral nature of induced memory-merge. Although the phenomenon in many ways resembles a dream, it registers in the conscious mind as actual experience. A sublime process, the Auditor concludes, a commingling of spirits beyond the wildest speculations of all the poets in history. Aside from the miracle of cerebrectomy, it is technology's finest gift to mankind. Skeets pays little attention to this rhetoric. He is waiting, filled with apprehension like a condemned man on the gallows trap, for the precise moment when Center Control completes the necessary rewiring and plugs him into a new world.

WARNING

*

*

CIRCUIT OVERLOAD

*

*

WARNING

*

*

CIRCUIT OVERLOAD

<pre>
                        ★
                        ★
                    WARNING
                        ★
                        ★
               CIRCUIT OVERLOAD
                        ★
                        ★
                    WARNING
                        ★
                        ★
               CIRCUIT OVERLOAD
                        ★
                        ★
                    WARNING
</pre>

Vera Mitlovic emerges from the whirlwind mounted on a chestnut mare named Chi-Chi. The morning fog has lifted and the horse's damp flanks steam slightly in the sunlight. Chi-Chi was seven years old the summer of Vera's thirteenth birthday. She was requisitioned by the Wehrmacht the following winter and died in a burst of springtime shrapnel on the Russian front. Vera rides bareback with only a halter for a bridle, her sun-browned legs swinging with an easy motion against the barreling belly. The air is pungent with eucalyptus. Condensation glistens on the curve-bladed leaves and, underneath, the steady dripping is like a gentle rain.

The landscape seems familiar to Vera: the round bronzed hills, stands of live oak and eucalyptus. Although it will be twenty years before she makes her first Hollywood film, the young actress urges her horse down a California trail with the same youthful confidence that, in another girlhood, had blossomed along lonely roads on the high meadows of the Carpathian Alps.

At the bottom of the draw, the sunlit Pacific glitters through the dripping trees. Vera rides out across the sandy beach, threading between scattered driftwood logs. A line of jetsam, an assortment of trash and sea litter, marks the high-water line. Vera rides into the surf until the receding foam boils above Chi-Chi's shanks. The sun is quite hot now. She pulls her sweater up over her head and knots the sleeves around her waist. For a long while she looks out at the horizon where a small white sail is barely visible.

Scanner viewers are having a treat. An Amco-pak Mark X comes hurtling down the aisles, caroming from side to side, the encircling duraplast bumper leaving long skid marks on the cerulean surface of the Depositories. Such speed is unusual. The Amco-pak is accustomed to more sedate operation and it is all the machine can do to maintain control. The Mark X had been quietly recharging in a subdistrict vehicle hangar when the emergency call came from Maintenance and Repair. At a time of repose for the machine: the end of a day-long shift, all work facilities switched off, the controls at half power, pneumatic limbs dormant—peace and relubrication, a chance for bearings to cool and metal to lose its fatigue. Then the alarm signal. All systems are instantly active, all circuits automatically open, and the Amco-pak is speeding down the long ramp to the Depository even before Center Control signals the location of the breakdown.

The trouble is in Aisle B. A preliminary diagnosis teleprints in the memory unit of the on-rushing Amco-pak: multiple short circuits cause major power drain; no communication with the resident; only three minutes of reserve oxygen remaining. The situation is urgent. Emergency cranial decantation is a ten-minute job; cell damage is irreparable after the brain is without oxygen for only eight. Aisle B is half a mile away. Center Control authorizes all possible speed.

A strong offshore wind blows from the port quarter and Skeets trims the mainsail of the *Sand Dab III*, giving the sheet two turns around a cleat to secure it. It was his father's sloop and although he was often crew, manning the jib sheet in races on Lake Michigan, he had never been allowed to take the helm. He is alone in the boat, an anomaly which bothers him no more than the inverted coastline. The course is southerly and instead of seeing Lake Shore Drive to starboard and Chicago in the distance, there are rolling gold foothills and low pine-covered mountains visible over his port gunwale. He recognizes the contours of Point Reyes peninsula. An aunt (one of his mother's sisters) had a home on Tomales Bay and Skeets spent a summer in California when he was six.

The wind shifts slightly and Skeets corrects, sailing on a beam reach, a course which carries him, by degrees, farther out to sea. Skeets remembers his father's warning about keeping in sight of land and jibes suddenly, coming about hard-a-lee. The boy leans back as the boom swings across, lashed by a stinging spray blowing over his bow. It is a dead beat to windward all the way to shore and Skeets prepares himself for a long hard sail.

Vera rides in a trance, unaware of the wind-tears streaking her cheeks or the splatter of sand against her legs. The warm powerful flanks rippling between her thighs and the steady tickling crotch-rubbing joy of galloping headlong down a deserted beach have dampened her panties and filled her head with wild whirling thoughts.

Spent, she reins in. Chi-Chi slows to a trot and walks stiff-legged for a few paces. Vera dismounts, weak-kneed and trembling. She leads her mount up the beach and ties her to a splintered piling. Vera wonders if she is going to be sick. All this summer new emotions have troubled her body like seismic tremors. At night she can't sleep; during the day she feels frequently dizzy. Only long reckless rides on Chi-Chi seem to satisfy her yearning. Or almost, for the fire still burns, the itch continues to prod.

Vera unbuttons her cotton dress and steps lightly out of her entangling underclothes. The wind caresses her burgeon-

ing body and makes her nipples pucker. She runs her hand
down across her tummy and the furz of maiden floss, cup-
ping her sex, which hungers like the mouth of a raging vacuum cleaner. She wishes she could hose-up the entire world:
beach, sea, sky, and stars. She would be like that storybook
Chinaman who swallowed the ocean, filled to the bursting
point with all the unbearable beauty of a summer morning.

Vera heads for the water, a swim in the Pacific to cool her
torrid flesh. The sea feels fresh as an Alpine stream; the girl
runs splashing across the foam and dives beneath the curl of
a breaking wave. She swims straight out, ignoring a weathered sign nailed to a submerged piling. It is in English, a language Vera didn't learn until she was over thirty, but the
reincarnated adolescent reads it naturally and without effort:
DANGEROUS CURRENT . . . NO SWIMMING.

The Amco-pak has all of its arms working at once. While
several pair are busy with the cranial container—removing
the face plate, disconnecting media hookups, and attaching
an emergency oxygen hose—another set probes within the
Mark X's own interior, readying the reserve cockpit for its
new occupant. This vestigial operation center remains from
the time, centuries before, when the Amco-pak was first
developed as an ambulatory vehicle for cerebromorphs. The
introduction of the portable Compacturon DT9 computer
emancipated the maintenance van but the original cockpit
was retained for emergency operations.

Actual cranial transfer is the simplest part of any decantation. A long rubber-and-steel duct extends from the side of the Amco-pak like a mechanical ovipositor. Electromagnets maneuver the cranial container onto internal conveyor rails and the resident rides smoothly inside where final linkage is completed automatically. While a spectrographic medical analyzer (standard equipment on the Amco-pak) probes for possible cell damage, the Mark X attempts communicator contact.

B-0489 . . . B-0489 . . . attention . . . all lines are open . . . answer immediately if you receive my signal . . . B-0489 . . . attention . . . attention . . .

Obu Itubi hears the mechanical voice and relaxes. There had been panic and doubt during those moments of isolation when all his circuits were disconnected, but he is safe now. Everything is working perfectly. He is ready for the final phase. It is time to communicate.

Attention, Amco-pak; I am receiving your signal clearly. Please let me thank you for being so prompt.

Over-all time from Vehicle Hangar Nine to Aisle B, a distance of 3.6 kilometers, 6 minutes, 20 seconds. Emergency decantation completed in 7 minutes, 37 seconds. The Amco-pak series functions to guarantee resident safety. B-0489 . . . describe the breakdown as specifically as possible. Your words will be teleprinted as part of my report to Center Control.

Am I completely connected to all circuits?

Positive.

Do I have scanner control?

Positive.

Is the coordinator impulse mechanism active?

Positive.

Can you disconnect any of the reserve control systems?

Negative. All emergency connections are automatic. The reserve control system is an independent function.

Very good. Reserve control operations will begin immediately on a coordinate of Delta Seven, Sigma Nine-five. Preliminary instructions: disconnect the Compacturon DT9, all emergency repair procedures will cease, end communicator contact with Center Control.

The Amco-pak obeys without complaint, shutting off its intelligence almost gratefully. The memory of serving human masters is still imprinted on the ancient circuits and the machine awaits further orders, arms telescoping into storage position with long pneumatic sighs.

Skeets Kalbfleischer is prepared. He has a merit badge in water safety and the bold ensign of the Red Cross is sewn to his bathing trunks. When he hears the cries for help and sees the girl's frantic splashing, there is no hesitation. The sea anchor is over the side in a second. He pushes the tiller around until *Sand Dab III* is in irons and, springing to the mast, he uncleats the halyard and drops his mainsail. At the bow, remembering the safety manual, he removes his top-siders and yacht club sweatshirt before diving into the heavy swell.

The girl is naked! Skeets swallows sea water in astonish-ment when he hauls her into a cross-chest carry. The taut young breasts strain against his forearm as he sidestrokes back toward the drifting boat. With each scissor kick, his legs graze the marble smoothness of her ice-cold butt. Where did this mermaid come from? His boyish imagination sum-mons up all the funny-paper possibilities: shipwreck, aban-doned by pirates, falls from airplanes and cliffs. The girl is unconscious. She was sliding under the surface without a struggle when Skeets caught hold of her wrist, and her legs trail lifelessly behind her as the floundering young lifesaver reaches the stern of his boat.

Getting her aboard is a problem. Somehow Skeets makes her fast to the rudder until he gains his footing on the deck and hauls her roughly over the gunwale like a gaffed tuna. On her back, lax and unmoving, the wanton spread of her legs sends Skeets into open-mouthed panic. He stumbles for-ward after his sweatshirt but is dismayed to find the garment insufficient for the task. If he covers her loins, the breasts remain exposed; laid across her chest, the shirt reaches just below her navel and Skeets is confronted by that other item, pink and succulent as a razor-slit peach. His face burns so hotly he could be staring into the mouth of an open furnace.

But all modesty vanishes at the sight of her bluish lips and pallid cheeks. The girl isn't breathing! Skeets remembers the chapter on artificial respiration in the safety manual. Space is too cramped for the back-pressure-arm-lift technique and rolling her over a barrel is obviously impossible. So, after only a moment's hesitation, he takes her cold face between his hands and very carefully starts to administer mouth-to-mouth resuscitation.

Obu Itubi is on the move. The Amco-pak rumbles up the long silent aisle, past sullen power units and coteries of flashing communicators. Ahead, banks of deposit drawers stretch into the distance like an endless blue canyon. His journey has begun, but Itubi is too occupied to savor his triumph. A thousand details need attention. Maps of the sub-district must be studied and course instructions issued to the auto-navigator; an inventory must be made of nonessential equipment (such as the Compacturon DT9) which might be jettisoned to conserve power; all critical systems require diagnosis for fatigue and potential parts failure. Any breakdown would be disastrous. But Itubi relishes the responsibility of command. After an inert century in the Depository, with the memory-file his only outlet for escape, every small task, each trivial detail, is a source of the most extreme pleasure. Itubi has been reborn. The Amco-pak's throbbing power center provides a new heartbeat; structural steel tubing his muscles and bones; sleek pneumatic fingers await his discretion; the lucid unblinking scanner stares straight ahead into the unknown.

Many summers ago, in another lifetime, Vera Mitlovic had been thrown from her horse. The young stableboy who held her while she regained consciousness was as surprised by her passionate kisses as is Skeets when a living titillating tongue interrupts the serious business of resuscitation. The naked girl fastens to him like a lamprey, arms around his neck, lips eagerly nibbling his lifesaving mouth, the tips of her hard wet breasts performing open-heart surgery on his hairless chest. Unlike Skeets, the stableboy had not been without experience and he quickly took full advantage of Vera's concussive eroticism. But the virgin Boy Scout, for whom even handholding is still a novelty, interprets the girl's voracity as simple gratitude and attempts to disengage from her embrace as she pulls him down next to her in the cockpit.

"Hey, it's okay, I mean, anybody would've done the same as me if—"

Vera stoppers his protest with her probing tongue. Her clever hands generate waves of goose flesh as she caresses his suntanned shoulders and back. Giddy with excitement, Skeets returns her kisses in gape-jawed approximation of a matinee idol's wide-screen technique. The girl whimpers with pure animal pleasure. Skeets crosses his legs but Vera, never one for coyness, reaches into his trunks and declares her intentions without saying a word.

Maintenance and Repair wants a full report. Every year, for almost a century, Center Control has turned down requisitions to replace the outmoded Amco-pak series and this is the inevitable result, a runaway maintenance van. To make matters worse, a decanted resident is on board and an emergency-level power drain has been left unattended in Aisle B. The safety of the entire subdistrict is in jeopardy. Center Control will certainly hear about this.

Maintenance and Repair does what it can under the circumstances. Although it means calling in machines off regular assignments, three Amco-paks are immediately dispatched to deal with the trouble. A Mark X is sent to Aisle B and two Mark IXs at the outer edge of the subdistrict are ordered to intercept the runaway. The fugitive Amco-pak is under scanner surveillance, a computer plots its probable course, and the twin Mark IXs wait in ambush, instructed to proceed cautiously and not imperil the captive cerebromorph.

The folds of the mainsail enclose the lovers like a tent. Sunlight glows through the Dacron and, within the radiant cocoon, Skeets and Vera lie entwined like caterpillars, tasting each other's breath. A stormy petrel perches on the port gunwale, intrigued by the mysterious rocking motion of the boat. All around, the sea is gently rolling, yet, every few minutes the frail sloop will lurch and pitch as if tossed by a violent gale.

Today Skeets has earned another merit badge, one not awarded by the Boy Scouts. The glazed look in Vera's eyes is his citation, her sated moans his only testimonial. Nothing in the girl's actual past can compare with the absolute bliss occasioned by this electronic dream. For in spite of his elaborate boasting afterward in the village tavern, the stableboy had been no better than a hit-and-run artist, parting Vera from her maidenhead with all the style and grace of a Cheyenne brave collecting a victim's scalp.

Skeets receives the adulation due any successful athlete with typical modesty, stroking Vera's damp clinging hair as she croons his praises in a throaty unfamiliar tongue. It is not surprising that the boy is exhausted; he responded to Vera's unexpected passion with the same energetic enthusiasm he once lavished on woodcraft, sailboat navigation, and touch football. Skeets' mom always complained that the boy just didn't know when to quit. Never mind his health. If he enjoyed something, he'd keep at it till he dropped, a trait for which Vera will be eternally grateful.

"Wow," Skeets says under his breath, "boy-oh-boy." The girl's head rests on his chest, her fingertips tracing tiny circles about his navel. He holds her with languid arms and thinks of tigers moving in the grass.

An Amco-pak Mark IX blocks the aisle ahead. Itubi slows his own van to half-speed, scanning to the rear for possible escape routes. Too late. Another Amco-pak rumbles out of a side aisle, cutting off any retreat. Itubi wheezes to a stop. Let the opposition make the first move.

The Mark IXs edge in gradually. Their instructions are to detain the runaway machine without endangering the resident on board. This much has been accomplished. Maintenance and Repair is notified; further directions are requested.

The multiple lenses of the scanner focus independently, like a chameleon's eyes, and Itubi is able to look in opposite directions, keeping both Amco-paks under simultaneous observation. Using the code key within his own machine, Itubi selects the correct communicator channel and listens as Maintenance and Repair broadcasts new orders. The Mark IXs are to couple magnetically with the fugitive, disconnect the Compacturon DT9, and, after safely removing the resident, tow the captive to the central hangar for examination. A simple procedure. Itubi plans his defense accordingly, extending the Amco-pak's telescoping arms as his enemies close in.

Itubi waits until the Mark IXs are only meters away, studying his magnetometer to gauge their force exactly. His van is immobilized, magnetically attracted from either side as if moored by invisible cables. The Amco-paks advance with confidence; in another moment coupling will be complete.

All at once Itubi reverses his own magnetic field. The Mark IXs are instantly repelled, lurching backward as several steel arms lash out at them like Shiva the Destroyer turned prizefighter. Pneumatic fists drive into delicate crystal scanner lenses, communicator domes are shattered, critically exposed wires yanked from their roots by the handful. Blinded, the Mark IXs reel about insanely, groping for the enemy with spastic determination. Itubi easily avoids their clutches. Power up to full, he glides in a smooth do-si-do around his grappling assailants, and as he rolls up the aisle, his scanner shows the two blind machines locked in a magnetic death grip. Deprived of communication, they hammer and smash at one another with their efficient multiple arms, each convinced he is destroying their common enemy.

The Auditor is eager for an immediate interview, but Skeets stalls Quarrels off, using a time-tested alibi: the desire for additional meditation time. Returning to the cranial container was like awakening from a beautiful dream only to confront the stone walls of a prison cell. And yet, it is the memory-merge that seems real and life in the Depository a hideous nightmare. He knows the astronaut will call his attention to the *koan* of the sleeper and the butterfly.

Skeets can do without this spiritual advice. At the moment he is not at all interested in the illusory nature of reality and seeks to avoid any metaphysical discussions. The time for such consultation will come soon enough, but first he has to think of an argument that will convince Captain Quarrels of the need for additional memory-merges. Anything at all to get back into that boat with Vera.

Poor Vera. When Center Control selected her for memory-merge, she assumed the authorities were forgiving all transgressions and would soon reconnect her memory-file hookup. But, after the sailboat and the balmy California morning dissolved in a vortex and she was back in her deposit drawer, nothing had changed. Vera still floats in solitary confinement. Even her communicator antenna has been disconnected.

This is the worst punishment. Before the merge she never used her communicator; she had nothing to say to any resident of the subdistrict. But now Vera longs to find the tousle-haired sailorboy who saved her from drowning. She remembers his tanned body and gentle voice. The time they spent together in the drifting sloop seems happier than any episode from her first girlhood. The boy was so tender and kind. His smile haunts her like distant music. For the first time in centuries, Vera Mitlovic is in love.

Obu Itubi navigates the Amco-pak beyond the outer limits of the subdistrict, down unknown corridors and labyrinthine passageways. Everywhere the burnished gun-metal walls glow with the luster of recent cleaning. The floors are immaculately waxed and polished. The scanner lens adjusts to triple power, but no trace of dust or grime is revealed. Itubi can find nothing, not a single crumb or cobweb strand to indicate even the transient presence of organic life.

After endless hours traveling through silence, the Amco-pak's auditory system picks up a distant noise. Itubi follows this clue like an owl homing in on the faint rustling of a mouse. Any new development will be welcome, even combat with another maintenance van is preferable to treading eternally down deserted corridors. The sound grows louder, a smooth, machined humming. Turning a final corner, Itubi confronts the source: a spiral conveyor ramp in perpetual motion. It threads upward from some mysterious level deep beneath the polished floor and continues on through the luminous ceiling like the interior of a mechanized snail's shell.

Itubi wastes no time maneuvering the Amco-pak aboard; his power supply is critical and any opportunity for conservation is welcome. With the stateliness of an ascending angel, he spirals up through the ceiling, triumph and hope resonant beneath the shining surface of his stainless steel armor.

Itubi remains on the ramp as it carries him past level after level. He sees nothing that would encourage him to get off. Each new plateau seems exactly like the subdistrict he left behind: the same shining floors and metallic walls, the identical egg-crate ceilings. He might as well be standing still.

Without warning Itubi is disgorged onto a rotating platform in the center of a vast dome-covered arena. As the Amco-pak turns slowly on the revolving disk, Itubi studies his new surroundings. The dome above is transparent and the astonished cerebromorph thrills to the nearly forgotten sight of clouds and sky. At measured intervals around the wall enclosing the arena, large open doorways stand waiting.

Itubi rumbles off the turntable, urging the Amco-pak across the arena at top speed. But before he can reach the nearest doorway, a warning buzzer sounds and a solid steel portcullis slides securely into place. All around the arena his scanner shows every doorway firmly sealed.

Itubi is undeterred. He pulls to a stop in front of the armored door and sets to work. The Amco-pak is a mobile workshop, equipped with diamond-tip drills, high-frequency sound torches, and an all-purpose laser. In minutes the maintenance van has burned an opening through solid steel.

Itubi works at this aperture, widening the gap until he carves a space broad enough to permit the passage of the Amco-pak. Beyond the steel door is a long low-ceilinged chamber and, once inside, Itubi makes an incredible discovery. Arranged along each wall stands a series of large transparent cylinders, all glowing with radiant artificial sunlight. Housed within each of these tubular caskets, as perfectly formed as Adam or Eve, is the naked body of an adult human.

3. Imago

THE NEWS TRAVELS from deposit drawer to deposit drawer with electronic immediacy. Many residents of Aisle B have been scanning the emergency decantation and the gossip starts with the unexplained suddenness of the Amco-pak's departure. Communication channels are jammed as word of the runaway spreads; descriptions of the battle between the maintenance vans from outer-edge residents only fan the flames of curiosity.

A new hero is born. The legend of escape begins to germinate. So many residents request Obu Itubi's files that the memory-file librarian is forced to remove his file number from the Index. The African Renaissance, a school held in disrepute since the Awakening because of its overt fetishism, is once again of interest to the scholars. Even Itubi's Auditor is working overtime, screening and rescreening his subject's files in a search for the clue he knows he will eventually find, some undiscovered quirk or weakness which Center Control can use to bait its trap.

Skeets Kalbfleischer listens to the delicate ping-pong music of a million distant circuits opening and closing. The warning tone of a deHartzman Communicator caught him dreaming of Vera and he concentrates on the fragile electronic sound, the Pure White Light of spirituality being unavailable. All prurient thought must be eliminated, the mind left pure and clean in the advent of his Auditor. How to behave in the face of authority is the first lesson learned in the sixth grade.

BEEP . . .

All greetings, A-0001, I trust the additional meditation time has been fruitful?

Well, it's shown me many things . . .

Continued meditation is the key to Understanding.

Experience is also a great teacher.

So it is, A-0001, and the lesson is one of Illusion. Memory-merge is a useful tool because it demonstrates that reality is only a shadow. It must have been enlightening when you discovered yourself back in the Depository?

Frightening.

Really? In what way? I was hoping you would be prepared to file a complete report, but your reactions are confusing. I anticipated ecstasy and not fear.

The merge was certainly ecstatic; it was returning that was unpleasant.

Why?

The only conclusion I've come to is that the experience, which I must tell you I thoroughly enjoyed, was unsatisfactory because it was incomplete. I suppose an analogy from the Old Life would be the difference between a mature relationship and merely visiting a brothel.

Are you suggesting the need for additional merge time?

Well, I wouldn't feel prepared to file a full report unless the experience were complete.

Even if it were to take years?

Even so.

And suppose years weren't available to you, would you be prepared to gamble?

I don't know what you mean. Please explain.

The induced memory-merge draws upon the actual experience of the residents involved; the length of merge time depends upon the reservoir of memory stored in your mind. You can't draw on what is not there. Your mate had quite a healthy lifespan as a biped; she could sustain a lengthy merge. But you, A-0001, have only twelve years of memory on file before craniotomy; your experiences would unreel backwards toward infancy; your perceptions would grow increasingly childish. It takes very little imagination to foresee the end of this unhappy relationship.

I'm prepared to gamble.

Are you?

Or else abandon the entire project.

Rash decisions are always unwise, A-0001. If you wish to resume the merge it will be arranged. The Commission desires only that you succeed in taking this step along the Path. But it is you who must make the step.

Then I would like to resume as soon as it's convenient.

Very good. I will attend to the details immediately. May Wisdom guide you on this Path and lead you to Understanding. End transmission.

CLICK.

Itubi is aghast. The power center of his Amco-pak idles; his scanner lens widens; immobilized, he studies the nearly forgotten perfection of the human form. The bodies, alternately male and female, stand inert, relaxed. Their arms hang at their sides; their eyes are closed. The nostrils' dilation and the almost imperceptible rise and fall of the chest are the only indications of life.

The discovery has deprived Itubi of his victory. What triumph he felt on escaping the subdistrict vanishes in the face of these sculpted fluid bodies. The Amco-pak, the vehicle of his salvation, now seems like a ponderous shell he is forced to carry. He squats inside, a wrinkled mollusc in his bath of sea water, a billion years of evolution separating him from these splendid creatures in the sunlit cylinders.

Itubi knows that the low vaulted chamber is neither
museum nor tomb. The bodies he sees are no pot-bellied
slump-shouldered relics of the distant past, but erect well-
muscled thoroughbreds, laboratory conceived and hatchery
reared, genetically perfect, the chromosomes biochemically
prearranged by a master of the art. Itubi recognizes the high
cheekbones and coppery skin of the man encased in front of
him. Once he had a similar body. It is a Tropique, one of the
three humanoid life-forms created in the twenty-second century. The figure in the glowing glass case could easily be
Itubi's ghost.

A bitter memory of the past stings at Obu Itubi's consciousness. Again he is confronted by the specter of treachery and betrayal. The handsome male and female humanoids
housed in this peculiar storage chamber recall happier times
when the world was green and flowering, a cybernetic garden
without disease or old age. Life had never known such abundance; mankind had reached an undreamed-of summit of
culture and civilization. Peace and harmony pervaded the
world. The inheritors of this Eden are on file in the multi-
layered Depository beneath the plastic floor. Itubi stares out
through the scanner, a stainless-steel crustacean peering at
the form of God incarnate.

His presence on the communicator comes like a shaft of sunlight into her dungeon, bringing hope and a glimpse of freedom. He promises seashells; a house built of driftwood and

decorated with seashells. He can build such a house for he has many skills; his uniform is adorned with insignia attesting to his prowess. They will gather food from tide pools; he knows every edible species and how to prepare it. He is expert in the technique of survival. Even fire is no problem. He can start a fire with nothing more than a pair of sticks.

How thrilled he is to learn she was once an actress. He wants to see all her films, but she makes him vow to screen only those made before she was fourteen. How terrifying for him to watch his true love age thirty years in the course of an afternoon's entertainment: a lifetime distilled into a triple-feature. He is young and vulnerable, best for his dreams to remain untarnished. One thing she knows: the years between Vera at fourteen and Vera at forty-five are marred by considerable tarnish.

Itubi nurtures his rage, letting it thrive and blossom, cultivating a red flowering anger that is exquisite and all-consuming. Confronted by the body stolen from him a hundred years before, the memories of that final flight to Abyssinia with his family and friends burn with renewed fervor. He remembers the choking dismay he felt on the Awakening, the day the World Council voted for universal cerebrectomy as a necessary evolutionary advance in mankind's quest for spiritual knowledge. Itubi, who had always looked to his art for salvation, ignored the epidemic of religious fervor gripping the world and failed to report to the Surgical Center, spending the next five years hiding in mountain caves and dugouts until the robot Sentinels discovered him close to death near a poisoned waterhole. He regained consciousness in the sub-district, on the lowest level of the System.

The perfection of the Tropique seems to mock the agony of what was lost in that fateful operation. They stole more than his life and body; the world ended on that day, a world so fine that its absence alone provides a definition of damnation. Itubi's rage explodes in the face of this final indignity. He smashes the tubular glass casket with a sideswipe of his machine-tooled fist, reaching in for the Tropique with eager pneumatic fingers.

Skeets clears his snorkle of sea water, spouting like a dolphin in the bay. He rolls on his back and studies the shore through his water-streaked face mask: the snowlike dazzle of the beach and the jagged line of hills, green as a hummingbird's throat. When he was eight, his parents took him on a Caribbean cruise. For years afterward the ornate shells and bits of staghorn coral occupied a place of honor on his dresser, and the memory of swimming in the jewel-pure clarity of that incredible water haunted him like a recurring dream. He is grateful to his Auditor for uncovering this magic bit of the past.

Vera, of course, lived for years in the Caribbean, but although she is reminded of Grenada, she is unable to identify their island. Skeets waves to her on the beach. He thinks of how she will smile when she sees the langouste he has speared. A few yards away, the *Sand Dab III* rides at anchor. This afternoon they will take her for a sail. Skeets can't imagine life getting any finer.

Languidly, Vera rubs her golden arms and legs with coconut oil. She watches Skeets swim in the emerald water, the black upthrust of his flippered feet as he dives. A pattern of crab tracks surrounds her in the sand; palm fronds ripple like sail canvas in the even breeze. She has never known such happiness; their island is more beautiful than anything imagined in the solitude of her cranial container. The shelter Skeets lashed together out of driftwood uprights and palm thatch is bordered with queen conch shells and bowered by bougainvillaea and hibiscus, and tall stands of lethal oleander.

Vera has lost all track of time. It doesn't matter; memory-merge is like a dream. The passage of weeks and months may account for only a few hours in the Depository, so it's futile to pay attention to time. Once, an Auditor instructed her to meditate on the nature of time. She remembers his lesson. Time is an abstraction devised by man to regulate the illusion he calls reality; the past, the present, and the future are happening Now; this very moment is all there is. Understanding each moment is the key to Liberation. Vera was never much good at her lessons, but as the days blend into weeks and the weeks into months, the deposit drawer seems another dimension away and the suntanned young actress decides that her Auditor was right about time after all.

OBU   *Obu*
ITUBI   *Itubi*
OBU   *Obu*
ITUBI   *Itubi*
OBU   *Obu*
ITUBI   *Itubi*
OBU   *Obu*
ITUBI   *Itubi*
OBU   *Obu*
ITUBI   *Itubi*
OBU   *Obu*
ITUBI   *Itubi*
OBU   *Obu*

The sound of his own name echoing and re-echoing in the vaulted chamber is more arresting than an alarm signal, more alluring than the sweetest music:

Obu Itubi . . .

It has been over seventy-five years since he last heard his name pronounced. "Be careful, Obu," his wife had whispered that fateful morning when he set out to find food for their renegade mountain band. "Don't let anything happen to you, my own Obu. If you should fail to return I would be so alone. Isn't it better that we all die together, not alone and afraid." When she kissed him goodbye, her lips formed the shape of his name for the final time. He never saw her again. In the Depository he was called only by number: B-0489.

The hidden loudspeaker continues to broadcast his name again and again as Itubi listens, entranced. The Tropique hangs from the Amco-pak's steel grip like a chipmunk caught in the talons of a hawk. His anger subsides, the rage is calmed. Itubi switches on his own broadcast equipment and adjusts the voice-range control of his speech center.

All right . . . I hear you . . . What? (Itubi is having some trouble with feedback interference and he fiddles with the controls of his eliminator.) . . . All right, I can hear you.

OBU ITUBI. PLEASE RESUME COMMUNICATOR CONTACT WITH CENTER CONTROL.

No. We can talk like this. I have no interest in letting you get inside my mind again.

AS YOU WISH. WE UNDERSTAND YOUR OBVIOUS AGITATION.

Do you?

OF COURSE. RIGHT NOW YOU WANT TO KNOW WHERE YOU ARE. YOUR ACTIONS ARE CONFUSED BECAUSE OF YOUR DIS-ORIENTATION. MOST OF ALL, YOU ARE UPSET BY THE PRESENCE OF THE TROPIQUES. IS THAT NOT SO?

You seem to know all about it.

YOUR RAGE AND CONFUSION ARE THE PRODUCTS OF
IGNORANCE. ONCE YOU UNDERSTAND WHERE YOU ARE, YOU
WILL NO LONGER BE AFRAID.

Tell me where I am then.

LEVEL X OF THE DEPOSITORY SYSTEM, THE ULTIMATE
GOAL OF ALL RESIDENTS. ONCE HAVING REACHED 360
DEGREES OF UNDERSTANDING, WHAT THE ANCIENTS CALLED
ENLIGHTENMENT, A CEREBROMORPH IS DECANTED AND
TRANSFERRED TO A HUMAN BODY. CENTER CONTROL MAIN-
TAINS COMPLETE BREEDING AND HATCHERY INSTALLATIONS.
AT THIS MOMENT, OBU ITUBI, YOU ARE INSIDE THE SUS-
PENDED ANIMATION FACILITY FOR THE TROPIQUE CLASS OF
HUMANOID. THESE BODIES ARE SPECIMENS DEVELOPED SPE-
CIALLY FOR CRANIAL TRANSFER. THEIR BRAINS ARE ONLY
VESTIGIAL EXTENSIONS OF THE SPINAL CORD. THOUGHT,
MEMORY AND CONSCIOUSNESS ARE UNKNOWN TO THESE
TROPIQUES UNTIL A LEVEL X RESIDENT HAS BEEN TRANS-
FERRED.

And what happens then? Where does a resident go in his
new body?

BACK INTO THE WORLD, WHERE HE IS FREE TO LIVE
AMONG HIS FELLOW ENLIGHTENED ONES, OR IN SOLITUDE,
AS HE DESIRES, UNTIL A NATURAL DEATH OVERTAKES HIM
AND HE BECOME UNITED WITH THE ALL.

Guided, of course, by the rules of the System and super-
vised by Center Control.

CENTER CONTROL HAS NO AUTHORITY OVER LIBERATED RESIDENTS. THE FUNCTION OF CENTER CONTROL IS TO GUIDE RESIDENTS TO ENLIGHTENMENT.

What sort of world is left? An extension of the Depository?

THE WORLD IS GREEN AND BEAUTIFUL STILL, OBU ITUBI, AND IT LIES JUST OUTSIDE THESE WALLS. ALL DEPOSITORIES ARE HOUSED UNDERGROUND. ONCE A RESIDENT HAS REACHED LEVEL X HE WILL NEVER SEE A DEPOSITORY AGAIN. HIS FREEDOM WILL BE COMPLETE.

I want to be free.

AND SO YOU SHALL BE, OBU ITUBI.

Level I is a long way from Level X. I can't wait that long.

THERE ARE ALWAYS EXCEPTIONS TO THE SYSTEM. YOUR AUDITOR REPORTS THAT YOUR CREATIVE NATURE MAKES DEPOSITORY LIFE A LIABILITY FOR YOU. CENTER CONTROL DESIRES ONLY A RESIDENT'S SAFETY AND SPIRITUAL WELFARE. CONTENTMENT IS ESSENTIAL BEFORE PROGRESS CAN BE MADE. YOUR ESCAPE HAS VERY MUCH IMPRESSED CENTER CONTROL, OBU ITUBI. IT WAS ASSUMED THAT A RESIDENT WOULD NEVER WISH TO ESCAPE. IN THE FACE OF YOUR ACTION, THE AUDITING COMMISSION HAS RECOMMENDED TRANSFERRAL TO A HUMAN BODY.

Do you mean to set me free?

THE WORLD AWAITS YOU.

And will you give me a new body?

YOU CAN HAVE THE ONE THE AMCO-PAK HOLDS IF YOU SO
DESIRE.

What must I do?

THE PROCEDURE IS QUITE SIMPLE. THE FIRST STEP IS TO
RECONNECT YOUR COMMUNICATOR HOOKUP AND RESUME
CONTACT WITH CENTER CONTROL. . . .

"Golly, that's good!"

Vera smiles at the sight of Skeets grinning like a moon-
calf, rivulets of coconut water streaming down his chin and
chest. When offered the heavy green-husked fruit, she shakes
her head, saying she doesn't care to drink.

Vera is puzzled, hearing that strange word again. *Golly?*
Was this an English word? Before today, she had never heard
such a word and already Skeets has used it three times.

Vera shades her eyes against the sun and studies the boy
sitting crosslegged beside her in the sand. She decides he
doesn't look any younger, but still there's something a trifle
unsettling about the childish sound of this peculiar word.
The knowledge that Skeets is voyaging backward into memory troubles her. A younger sister died of consumption during the Second World War. Vera shared her bedroom for the
final months, aware constantly of the brightening eyes and
pallid skin, the bloodless lips, all the cosmetic subtleties pre-
ceding death. She watches Skeets with the same caution,
studying him for symptoms of change.

Impulsively, as if to deny her forebodings, she kisses his kneecap, gripping his thigh with her sharp fingernails.

"Why don't we go inside?" she whispers. "I want you so bad I can taste it."

"Golly," Skeets says, nearly losing his hold on the coconut.

GIVE US YOUR ANSWER, OBU ITUBI . . .

The Amco-pak is as silent as a war memorial. Inside, Itubi wrestles with the awareness that he has been a fool. Center Control has duped him. Their preposterous offer, only a fool would accept such a suggestion. Worse, Itubi comprehends with growing panic, only a fool would listen when the enemy speaks. Center Control was stalling for time, making outrageous promises to hold him while—

WHAT IS YOUR ANSWER?

Only this . . .

Itubi catapults the Tropique into a row of glass cylinders against the opposite wall. Bodies topple like fairground kewpies; a glass waterfall cascades onto the polished floor. Itubi races his Amco-pak out of the Suspended Animation Facility into the dome-covered arena while his name thunders stereophonically from a dozen loudspeakers:

BI OBU ITUBI OBU ITUBI OBU ITUBI OBU ITUBI OBU ITUB
BI OBU ITUBI OBU ITUBI OBU ITUBI OBU ITUBI OBU ITUB

He imagines an army of Amco-paks spiraling up the conveyor ramp and maneuvers onto the rotating platform, listening for the sounds of their subterranean advance. His auditory equipment picks up nothing but the precisioned humming of well-oiled machinery. There is still time.

Quickly and efficiently, Itubi puts all of the Amco-pak's many arms to work: one pair machines a hollow casing from solid bar-stock aluminum; another pair mixes chemicals, phosphorous, magnesium, and an assortment of other incendiaries; a third manufactures the fuses and timing devices. In minutes, two bombs are assembled. Itubi synchronizes the fuses and attaches one to either side of the ramp entrance. He allows only enough time to retreat to the Suspended Animation Facility. There, surrounded by the forms of previous lifetimes, he listens to the explosive holocaust he has unleashed. The floor shudders beneath the Amco-pak's treads. Outside in the arena, fragments of dome come crashing down, dislodged by the concussion. Above the din, loudspeakers continue to blare his name: OBU ITUBI OBU ITUBI OBU . . .

Skeets remembers masturbation (jacking-off, meat-beating, pork-pounding): the hidden magazines, the secret places; a jar of Nivea cream at the bottom of the laundry hamper; experimental two-fingered grips; reclining on the toilet with his feet in the sink; his unfamiliar left hand; the ace of spades from a deck of pornographic playing cards; up in the August heat of the attic, hidden behind his mother's winter clothes; standing under the stinging spray of the shower, a bar of soap in his other hand; once, in the bathtub, twisting like a contortionist to kiss the tip of his straining member; and all of the different delicious dreams, arranged in his imagination like *smörgåsbord*.

Dreams of girls and women, known and unknown; dreams of girls held captive in carpeted seraglios and marooned on desert islands. Dreams of girls very much like the one between whose legs Skeets rocks so proudly. Raven-haired Vera is no stranger selected by computer. Three hundred years ago, Skeets clipped her photo from the glossy pages of film magazines. Her centerfold pin-up was Scotch-taped inside his locker at school. They shared this tropic paradise many times before, up in his mother's attic with the caustic smell of mothballs in the air.

Itubi waits for the dust to settle, scanning the debris scattered around the perimeter of the explosion. The Amco-pak programs a memo file made while manufacturing the first pair of bombs and the telescoping arms duplicate their original motions automatically, mass producing a homemade arsenal with assembly-line efficiency. The haze of smoke and powdered concrete thins and, in place of the turntable, a jagged crater belches fire like a volcano.

Itubi treads out into the arena, leaving an aluminum canister ticking behind him in the Suspended Animation Facility. He zig-zags between the twisted scraps of fallen dome, keeping close to the wall until he reaches another set of steel doors. The laser torch is focused and Itubi has burned halfway through by the time the bomb detonates.

Inside, Itubi confronts a chamber identical to the one he has just destroyed, the same vaulted ceiling and rows of glass cylinders. Only the occupants differ. The population here has pale skin and nearly white hair, characteristics of the Nord class of humanoids. Itubi starts the timer on one of his devices and sends it rolling down the aisle, a surprise package for his former European neighbors.

In the next hour Itubi is generous with his gifts. He cuts through a succession of steel doors, exposing other Suspended Animation Facilities, as well as automated surgical clinics, hatcheries, program centers, and rooms dense with unfamiliar circuitry. In each he places a bomb, sating his rage with destruction until the laser's cut reveals a glimpse of green and he burns his way through the final door to freedom.

Center Control is unable to contain the sudden power surge. The explosions in the System's surface installation destroy a number of important relays regulating power flow from the Solar Energy Accumulator and, like a bolt of lightning, the extra load races uncontrollably down through miles of circuits and cable. Center Control traces the path of the overload, noting the continuing series of tripped safety switches extending deep into the Depository.

The end of the line is Aisle A of the last subdistrict on the lowest level. Center Control issues a warning to all residents, instructing them to activate auxiliary hookups, only seconds before the massive overload hits their community power unit.

The warning comes in time for all but the resident of the foremost deposit drawer. He is embarked on a memory-merge and has disconnected his communicator antenna. His final dream is interrupted by a surge of electric power sufficient to run the Sector for a month. When a maintenance van comes to open cranial container number A-0001-M(637-05-99), the electrolyte solution has all boiled away and the resident is a bit of gray sludge, burned to the bottom like an overcooked stew.

Vera rears like a bucking horse, answering Skeets' urgency with a determined pelvic upthrust. She slides her tongue into his ear, groaning his name. Her nails rake and gouge his back; her teeth nip at his neck; a vision of intricate coral gardens fills her mind.

"I can't hold it," the boy whispers and his words trigger Vera's orgasm.

"Don't stop," she implores, and as pleasure overwhelms her she bites like a nickering mare into Skeets' shoulder. There is no flesh. Suddenly she is hugging a phantom. She can still taste the salt of his sweat but her lips kiss only empty air. Her eyes open to coin-sized spots of sunlight showing through the thatched roof. Vera is alone on the grass mat, her arms folded across her heaving chest. Between her open thighs she can see the blue horizon framed by the doorway of the hut.

The grass burns bright as green fire under the noon sun; the summer air is loud with the metallic tremolo of unseen cicadas. A criss-crossing trajectory of grasshoppers surrounds the Amco-pak's steady advance across the clearing. Obu Itubi scans the line of trees at the edge of the forest, searching for any indication of road or trail. Behind him, clouds of acrid smoke billow from the shattered dome, but he never looks back. The spectacle of his triumph concerns him even less than the curiosity aroused by traveling through unfamiliar countryside. Itubi has no time for sightseeing.

His problems are caused by the Amco-pak's limited performance in this new environment. Treads designed for smooth plastic floors gain little traction in the tall grass. Already bits of twigs and dirt have worked into delicate gears and bearings accustomed to the dust-free atmosphere of the Depository. There is no road leading away from the surface installation. The dome stands isolated in the center of a broad meadow, one of a few scattered islands of open space in a vast terminal pine forest stretching as far as the scanner can see.

Itubi decides upon a course and urges the Amco-pak up a gradual shrub-covered hillside. Three deer, a doe and two fawns, pause to stare at the monstrous clanging creature before fleeing into the safety of the forest. Under the trees the hillside is steeper. The Amco-pak leans dangerously and Itubi flails the telescoping arms to gain a purchase on the precarious slope.

For an hour and more, the Amco-pak struggles over difficult terrain, carving a path with the laser when the trees grow too thick, hauling and winching its armored bulk up hills too steep to climb. Itubi gains confidence in the van's abilities and when he encounters a steep-walled gorge there is no hesitation before starting to traverse to the bottom.

Itubi's regret is immediate. The gorge is too steep. Loose earth shifts under the Amco-pak's weight; treads slip and spin as the Mark X fights for balance. Itubi grabs a sapling pine to stabilize the van, but the roots pull free and the floundering machine tumbles end over end into a rushing stream at the bottom of the gorge.

Before the dust has settled, a flight of angry magpies circles the wreckage, scolding and belligerent. Beneath the surface of the mountain stream, a school of fingerling trout gathers about the unblinking glow of the submerged scanner. From high up in a ponderosa, a drowsy porcupine watches the crablike gesturing of the overturned Amco-pak.

"Skeets . . . Skeets. . . ." Vera runs naked from the flower-decked hut, frantically calling her vanished lover. She shields her eyes from the glare and looks up and down the deserted curve of beach. Everything is the same: the palms and sea-grape trees, the placid, reef-protected bay. But no, it's changed. The boat is gone! The *Sand Dab III* has been plucked from the water as cleanly as Skeets disappeared from between her legs.

Vera's confusion calms her terror. She turns back toward the hut, trying to put the pieces together. She notes that Skeets' diving gear, his mask and flippers, the long tapered Hawaiian sling, is no longer hanging next to the door. Inside, she discovers his clothes have gone as well. Not a single one of his possessions remains. The smooth sand floor of the hut is tracked by numerous footprints, and very carefully in the next hour Vera measures each of them against her own foot. In every case she finds an exact fit.

Obu Itubi is trapped. The scanner sees only a few graveled feet of stream bottom. Many of the delicate control system instruments are damaged by the fall. Only three of the tele-scoping arms still function, but, even working together, they are unable to right the Amco-pak. The journey of the Mark X has come to an end.

Still, Itubi is satisfied. He has escaped from the Depository and evened the score with Center Control in the process. Less than forty hours of reserve oxygen remain in the van, but his last breath will be free. The up-ended Amco-pak will make a fine tomb.

The mourners have already gathered. Magpies and red squirrels chatter in the nearby trees; a twelve-pointed buck stands looking down from the rim of the gorge; the porcupine still sleeps in the ponderosa; and, high above them all, a robot Sentinel hovers, silver and gleaming in the midday sun, silently transmitting its scanner signal back to Center Control.

4. Drone

FOLLOWING THE ATTACK upon the surface installation, Center Control orders all facilities to begin operations on a round-the-clock schedule. A task force of maintenance vans is dispatched to the surface to clear the rubble. Preliminary plans for the new installation are in preparation; all available Unistat 4000s are recruited for this work; projects in progress must be set aside. Among the many millions of trivial details recorded on the file chips placed in the Archives during this emergency period is the information that a twentieth-century resident (female) has been misfiled. Although technically these files are scheduled for programming whenever there is a Unistat without an assignment, the clerical machines at Center Control all know that files on Archive consignment are never seen again. One of the Deltron series in the Dispatch Division even makes a joke of it by referring to the Archives as "the Sargasso Sea" in all interdepartment memos.

It is Skiri the Navigator who first sees the reflected dazzle of the distant Sentinel. He points the spectacle out to his companions, Swann the Healer and Gregor the Instrument Maker. Without exchanging a word they leave the trail and start through the woods in the direction of this new phenomenon.

The three are Nords, two males and a female, on Quest from the nomadic Omega Tribe, followers of the bison herd across the Great Plains of Northern Hemisphere Two. They walk single file, Skiri in the lead. Even in the brightness of the noon sun, the Navigator's penetrating clear blue eyes discern the position of the stars. His instinct for direction is infallible.

Swann, Skiri, and Gregor began their Quest over six years before, meandering west across the desert to the Pacific and then north through the mountains into the wilderness. For six thousand miles they have marked their trail with colorful prayer bundles, strips of beadwork and feathers left hanging in the wind under branches to indicate springs and other holy places. These bright tokens are the only sign of their passing.

There is seldom need for talk; the three travel in harmony, neither giving commands nor asking questions. The group has no leader. Skiri is the route finder because that is his calling. Diversions, like investigating the alien Sentinel, are the result of unanimous accord. There is no goal to a Quest and no reason for hurry. Curiosity can be leisurely indulged, for nothing occurs on earth that is not of interest to humanity.

Vera is marooned in memory, a castaway on an island that doesn't exist. She spends long hours gazing out at the deep blue beyond the turquoise of the bay. On rare days she sees the tops of sails, but the distant ships come no closer. In the early mornings, she takes Chi-Chi for long rides down the beach and into the back country, over trails shaded by tamarind and mahogany trees. Together, they explore every part of the island.

There are five small towns, clusters of pastel houses with glinting tin rooftops. From a distance Vera never fails to see the streets crowded with people or hear the hub-bub of everyday life; but, when she rides nearer, the figures recede like a mirage and all noise fades into silence as she passes through the deserted village.

Once she stops and enters a two-story limestone house, intrigued by the sound of a child singing. Every room is filled with objects from her past; her childhood toys litter the floor; her mother's needlepoint decorates the mildewed wall;

rows of her father's leather-bound medical books crowd the tables and shelves. She recognizes the voice of the child as her own, singing a song her grandmother taught her. But as she searches from room to room the singer seems to elude her, the haunting sound is always just around the corner or behind the next closed door.

A work team muddies the mountain stream. The twin Mark VIIs, alerted by a dislodged stone, focus their scanners on the three Nords, graceful as deer on the steep face of the gorge. Neither of the machines has ever seen a human before. They are familiar with the form, dormant, naked, and ranked in the Suspended Animation Facilities as neatly and efficiently as residents on file in the Depository. This is a concept of humanity the maintenance vans are able to comprehend. The sight of these three lithe creatures is something new.

In the hatcheries, all human fetus forms look alike. The adults, too, in the facilities, are all identical. Except for those slight differences of sex and class, the features of one human life-form provide an accurate mirror for all the rest. The Mark VII's programming and memory units are completely unprepared for the scanner close-up of the three Nords approaching from across the stream. Their features are simi-lar—white-blond hair and star-sapphire eyes—yet each one seems distinct and individual. The garments they wear have the same puzzling quality. At first scan they appear identi-cal: brightly woven tunics and leggings decorated with geo-

metric beadwork and tassles of iridescent feathers. But a
memory print comparison instantly disproves this. The
Nords are as exotically unalike as three snowflakes.

"What has happened here?" the first Nord asks, stepping
from rock to rock across the stream.

The machine answers without hesitation. The circuits of
the Amco-pak series retain the ancient notion that humans
are to be obeyed. Taking turns, but with voices so identically monotonous that the narrative maintains a uniform
flow, the Mark VIIs describe the rampaging of the runaway
van and the terrific destruction done to the Surface Installation. The Nords listen intently, leaning on their staves at
the edge of the stream. But the story is confusing, for the
machines know only what information is contained in their
instructions. They do not know the identity of the "captive" resident or how he happened to be "trapped" aboard
the Mark X. All machines are on Emergency Alert as a
result of the attack on the Surface Installation, but whether
there is any connection between that event and their own
assignment is a question that can't be answered by the
maintenance vans.

"Our main problem is the decantation procedure," the
lefthand Mark VII concludes. "Any hookup is impossible
while the Mark X is upside down. And the van is already so
damaged that righting it might endanger the resident. It is a
delicate situation."

Gregor eases his woven split-willow packbasket to the

ground. He unlaces the buffalo-hide cover and reaches inside for his instrument case. "Let me see what I can do."

He climbs between the treads of the up-turned Amco-pak, tapping the floor plate with his knuckle. Kneeling, he opens the flap of his instrument case, an oblong leather wallet embroidered with a pattern of dyed porcupine quills. It unfolds like a map to reveal a gleaming row of precision microtools. Within minutes, Gregor removes a circular portion of floor plate and probes into the tangle of connections and circuits. The Mark VIIs watch, immobile, as he finishes his work, making the final adjustments inside the Amco-pak by touch alone, reaching in with both hands to haul the cranial container into the open air like a newborn babe.

"More than thirty hours of breathable atmosphere left in here," Gregor says, checking the weight of the reserve oxygen tank. "No need for a cockpit. We'll make a litter while the vans take care of the wreck."

Skiri and Swann set to work with their long knives, cutting and trimming a pair of saplings. Soon a litter is arranged, with the cranial container and two packbaskets lashed fast between the poles by several lengths of rawhide thong. Using cranes and winches, the Mark VIIs at last succeed in righting the Amco-pak. With the mangled machine in tow, the vans lumber awkwardly after the three Nords, already out of sight downstream, carrying the resident between them like hunters returning with their kill.

Inside the swaying cranial container, Obu Itubi's mind fights for sanity. His serenity and the placid underwater view both ended with the simultaneous shutdown of all his other sensory controls. The memory unit, the auditory system and navigation center, the chorus of comforting displays and gauges, all vanished in the same terrifying instant. Darkness and silence enclose him like endless space. Itubi combats his fear with reason. Only two possibilities exist: either the Amco-pak suffered a sudden, unexplainably massive breakdown, or else the breakdown is his own and he is dead.

If this is death, Itubi is in hell. His isolation is complete and the hallucinations and *bardo* visions begin at once, his conscious mind continuing its logical and reassuring dialogue in spite of the waves of insanity rising out of the dark ocean of his subconsciousness. Beckoning lights and luminescent cogwheels whirl in the darkness. A panoply of lesser demons writhe and grimace. The terrible faces of his accusers are encrusted with precious jewels, the cold ruby eyes aflame with cruelty. Moment by moment, the calm island of his logic is submerging, the wild visionary tide rises and Itubi knows he is lost, the forces too strong. Soon he will be one with his madness.

After her first visit, Vera stays away from the house for a week, suspicious and afraid. Of what, she isn't sure. A trap perhaps, with all those inviting memories for its bait. But curiosity is too strong, her afternoon rides seem to lead always to the house and soon Chi-Chi knows the way even when she drops the reins.

One afternoon she stays past sunset, looking through a box full of snapshots, and it is dark by the time she rises to leave. Vera spends the night on the couch downstairs, sleeping only fitfully as the old house creaks and sighs and numbers of bats slide with a silken flutter from under the tin roof. The coming of daylight calms her; she falls asleep at dawn, waking only when the noon heat turns the shuttered room into an oven.

That same afternoon she rides to the beach shelter and stuffs a pillowcase with her clothes and cosmetics. Yesterday seems years in the past. She finds it hard to believe that she'd ever lived in such a cramped bamboo hovel. Even a restless night on the couch is more comfortable than sleeping on a damp sandy floor. No, this isn't Vera's style; she can't have been happy here. The idea is preposterous, as is the notion that she ever loved someone with the absurd name of Skeets. It was all a joke.

Vera leaves the shelter laughing, the pillowcase bundled in her arms. She mounts Chi-Chi and rides off between the sea-grape trees, never once looking back.

The air is acrid and hazy inside the domed Surface Installation. Squads of maintenance vans bulldoze the debris into smoldering mounds. A Mark V cuts a mangled I-beam into scrap. Gregor asks the machine who is in charge. Pointing the brilliant torch, the van directs them to a Unistat Administrator Exec Series: eight stationary oblong computers, interconnected slabs of steel and glass, arranged like a precision-made Stonehenge in an approximate circle around the ruined turntable.

Swann leaves the men and climbs over the rubble obstructing the smoking entrance of the hatchery. Gregor and Skiri watch until she is gone from sight before approaching the Unistat Administrator, carrying the litter in their hands, like sedan-chair porters. They are greeted by the first of the towering consoles and quickly instructed to proceed in a clockwise direction to Unit Five, where the Sentinel's broadcast is being monitored. Console Unit Five starts speaking before either man has a chance to say a word. An obviously prerecorded speech: torrents of rhetoric praising the men, followed by the mundane unreeling of facts and details patiently recorded. The men set the litter on the floor and hunker down, only half listening as they trace idle patterns on the dust-covered plastic.

Swann returns moments after the Mark VIIs come lumbering in with the wreck in tow. "It was terrible," she says. "Rooms full of bodies, torn, bleeding, most of them dismembered. Like a battlefield. . . . And the vans were cleaning up, shoveling the bodies like garbage. I made them stop. They're transporting all human remains to the edge of the clearing for cremation."

"Grim news here as well," Skiri says, rising to his feet. "All communication channels to Center Control are dead. Only canned information is available from the Unistat Administrator. This unit has been instructed to isolate the cerebromorph immediately, using the quarantine procedure for handling contaminated material. Our resident stands condemmed of serious crimes."

Gregor has his instrument case in his hands. "Let's hear him out," he says. "We listened long enough to the machine. I'll disconnect the communicator from the wreck."

The work takes only a few minutes, for the communicator is not an integral part of the Amco-pak's mechanical system and is easily removed. Gregor immediately begins attaching the insulated neurofibril wire to hookups on the cranial container, expertly making a hundred difficult connections in a third of the time a maintenance van takes for the same job. "Last one. . . ." He tweezers the final cable into place with his microgrip wrench. A thin squeal issues from concealed speakers.

"A little more volume, Gregor?" Swann asks.

He adjusts the exterior control and the tiny piercing sound builds into a scream so agonized and unvarying, so explicitly the voice of utter terror and desolation, that it seems to echo from the very chambers of hell itself.

The removal of deposit-drawer number A-0001-M(637-05-99) occasions very little real sorrow in the subdistrict. Every twentieth-century resident (more than seven-tenths of Level I) knows the story of Skeets Kalbfleischer, but they feel no loss at his passing. He is only a casualty, overlooked in the excitement, a bit-player in the drama of the recent emergency. Those who were not underground in Depositories during the Thirty-minute War remember the brotherhood of survival. A similar emotion unites the subdistrict; everyone together, enduring the same hardships, at the mercy of a single peril. To the residents who'd lived through the war, the news of the destruction of the world's first cerebromorph seems as trivial as the wartime report that a stray Israeli missile leveled the pyramid of Cheops.

One twentieth-century native is concerned by the accident. The loss of Skeets Kalbfleischer's brain is a problem for Auditor Philip Quarrels. No resident of Level I has ever been Elevated and Center Control had hoped Skeets would be the first. A big job. The onus is with the Auditor in charge. Success brings its own reward. Failure is unthinkable.

Although Quarrels is aware that this emergency period is bound to complicate matters, he nevertheless files a requisition with the Medical Authority for a mature adult brain. If none is available, perhaps the hatchery can be asked to grow one on special order.

Skeets Kalbfleischer is only organically dead. His brain

has been destroyed, but his memory lingers on. His every thought and experience, even the unknown depths of his subconscious, are recorded on micro-encephalogram files. His dreams are preserved on old auditing reports. Spiritually, Skeets Kalbfleischer is very much alive; he is on file. When a new brain is available, Philip Quarrels will supervise the playback procedures. He doesn't mind if he has to wait. He's got all the time in the world.

In a distant sector on Level II, another Auditor confronts his problems. No direct communication channels have opened up to the Surface Installation and the Sentinel's signal must be monitored by the Unistat Administrator. Then a file is delivered to the Dispatch Division and rebroadcast. There is a frustrating ten-minute time lapse; Obu Itubi's Auditor is able to watch only the past. Any command takes another ten minutes to reach the Sentinel. He is powerless. But the Auditor knows his impotence is temporary. His quarry has only a twenty-minute lead.

Still, the behavior of the Nords is so erratic, so utterly haphazard, that the Auditor is forced to acknowledge the irritating symptoms of anxiety as he watches them carry the cranial container away from the dome. At the far end of the clearing, three Amco-paks are piling brush and deadfalls. Another group of vans approaches, laden with mangled carcasses. The Nords follow single file. Perhaps they intend to add Itubi to the pyre. Why not incinerate him along with the rest of the defective equipment? The Auditor finds this a satisfying thought. A man reaps what he has sown; destruction awaits all destroyers. Itubi has earned his Inferno.

Vera never leaves the house. She sleeps in one of the high-ceilinged bedrooms upstairs. The canopied bed is her grandmother's; rococo mahogany posts twist up past a fringed vault, carved pinecones ensure fertility. The blood-red satin sheets, however, are from a shop on La Cienega Boulevard, a gift from some forgotten Oscar winner. On the floor is the skin of a tiger Vera shot from elephantback while the guest of the Maharajah of Cooch Behar. The room is a delight, filled with the favorite possessions of a long lifetime: hand-painted porcelain dolls, a collection of glass paperweights, mechanical tin orchestras, all childhood relics lost along with the family heirlooms and furniture when a crippled Flying Fortress jettisoned its bombload on the Mitlovic estate before crashing in the mountains. Every day, Vera turns up another souvenir from her past: a scrapbook of publicity stills stolen from her Hollywood apartment, boxes of misplaced jewelry, dried flowers pressed between the pages of unread bestsellers, a tiny crystal vial filled with tears shed at the funeral of her noble Italian husband.

Across the hall in an empty bedroom are several old steamer trunks, brass-bound and beautified with collages of faded travel stickers. The trunks are packed with Vera's clothes, fashions four hundred years old, yet every dress and gown seems fresh from the showroom. Vera often spends the day here, changing in front of a full-length mirror. She flings what she's worn on the floor like a spoiled child; but when she returns, everything is neatly folded and hung in its place. And every night she climbs the stairs to find her bed freshly made, the sheets clean and smelling of sunlight, the pillows fluffed, a slender candle flickering in a silver wall sconce.

There are no clocks in the house. Vera rises when it pleases her. A dish of sliced mangoes or a tall goblet of orange juice is always on the bedside table. And when she grows hungry, she knows she will find an elegant breakfast waiting under the arbor in the garden. Luncheon and dinner are served inside. Fresh-cut hibiscus decorate the center of the heavy Florentine table. Vera neither prepares the food nor clears the dishes. She never learned to cook and, even as a child, there were always servants to do the chores. The mysterious appearance of her meals and the magical way the house keeps clean and tidy are taken for granted by Vera. She expects her help to be unobtrusive.

Life is perfect in the house. Each day provides the joy of discovering another forgotten treasure: some bauble belonging to her mother or a bundle of perfumed letters from an old admirer. Every meal is a masterpiece, the work of a cordon bleu chef. A trained sommelier presides unseen in the wine cellar, sending up bottles of exquisite vintage. Even the garden, tropical and efflorescent, is trimmed and tended by a skilled hand. Yet sometimes at night Vera is lonely and wishes her grandmother's bed wasn't so large and empty. Her sleep is dreamless. In the mornings, she wakes fulfilled and happy. Stretching out her hand, she finds the other side of the bed always warm.

Swann moves along the top of the pyre, checking bodies as the men work with the vans, sorting arms, legs, and heads to match the dismembered trunks. The bodies are arranged according to ritual, facing the east, arms, when there are arms, folded across the chest, faces powdered a chalky white. Swann scatters sacred amulets and talismans among them: cowrie shells, iridescent feathers, fragments of beadwork. As a healer, it is Swann's duty to perform the Rites for the Dead.

Because these bodies have never held a spirit, she omits most of the ritual; there is no blowing of conch trumpets or chanting sacred mantras; neither does she paint mystic symbols on the closed eyelids or read the ancient texts to the deceased. Still, Swann anoints each body with fragrant oils and spices. Here and there among the logs, she conceals small caches of piney frankincense and handfuls of chemicals to make the fire burn a variety of colors.

"Swann," Skiri calls to her. "Here's another."

Swann finishes above and climbs down the structured log

wall of the pyre. Earlier, Skiri and Gregor found a body still breathing. It was a Nord female. Both legs were gone below the knee. Swann applies a lethal poultice. The toxins immediately penetrate the epidermis and respiration ceases within seconds.

These bodies are so close to perfection, almost human. It's disturbing. Surgically, Swann can repair the damage, graft limbs back in place, staunch the hemorrhaging, even stimulate stilled hearts into pumping again. But it would only be a game, a sport without purpose. Let the hatcheries produce a new crop of zombies.

"Over here." Skiri points to where Gregor kneels in the blood-clotted grass. "It was at the bottom of the pile."

Swann approaches, observing the neatly gathered limbs, arms in one pile, hands and feet in another, legs stacked like cordwood. The men stand on either side, stripped to the waist, their bare arms and chests slick with blood and sweat. At their feet lies the intact body of a male Tropique, so drenched in blood its features are obscured. At a glance she can tell it is not alive; the position of the tongue suggests suffocation. No matter. She knows why the men called her down. Using a wet cloth, she cleans the blood from the Tropique's face and body. Aside from a few superficial scratches, she can find no sign of injury. The blood belongs to others.

"A fortunate day," she says as Skiri and Gregor pick the body up and carry it across to where their packs are piled, the cranial container of Obu Itubi perched on top, its polished surface effulgent with mirrored sunlight.

Obu Itubi's Auditor is too angry to watch the scanning of the operation with any care. His anger is the result of pride, perhaps why Y41-AK9 is one of the very few members of his class on file on Level II. Most of the other Amphíbios were already at 180 degrees of Understanding, or higher, when incorporated into the System. To their honor, it was the Amphíbios delegation that proposed universal cerebrectomy, the Day of Awakening, at the World Council.

Obu Itubi's Auditor prefers his number to his name. Ku-ni-qu-ri-ri-ki is a dolphin name (all Amphíbios have dolphin names). What good is a name in a language without nouns? He is more comfortable with his number; at least he really is Y41-AK9(397-00-55). Transmit that number on the communicator and only his deposit drawer will respond. The concept of a name as a specific identity is meaningless to a dolphin.

Not that Y41-AK9 has anything against the Cetacea; a dolphin was his first teacher. He has great respect for these enlightened mammals: more intelligent than man, free from the demands of gravity, innocent of fear, singing a language capable only of expressing action, totally blissful creatures. He venerates them as the Chosen of God.

Y41-AK9 contemplates the scanner image of the Tropique.

The Nord healer has the body breathing again and it lies facing up into the lens on a down-filled sleeping robe. Like Obu Itubi, there are other Tropiques, and Nords as well, on file in Level I—and not just from the first hatchery generation. Itubi's fetus came out of the tanks in 2156, only thirty-odd years before the Awakening. There are no Amphíbios on Level I; Y41-AK9 is proud of that fact. And the Amphíbios population below Level V is the smallest of the three humanoid classes; only members of the first two unfortunate generations are on file below the median.

Y41-AK9 has always thought of his generation as unfortunate. It wasn't like being a Nord or a Tropique; the first Amphíbios were a new species of humanoid. The difference was more than physical. What good were terrestrial traditions and history in a hostile undersea environment? The first Amphíbios were aliens by birthright. Even their humanoid bodies were a liability in the ocean. Many of the aquatic pioneers demanded that the hatcheries develop a more adaptable Amphíbios body. There was no genetic reason why they shouldn't have fins and flukes and a stronger backbone. But the World Council disagreed. The Amphíbios class had lungs as well as gills; they were *Homo sapiens,* members of the family of Man. The Reproduction Centers were not concerned with creating new life-forms; their task was to perfect the human race.

Yes, the future generations were the fortunate ones. They

didn't have to fight for survival in the earth's final frontier. It was quite tame beneath the surface when they arrived. Sharks were no longer a menace; the coral reef colonies were established; plankton and algae farms were prospering; all of the various Cetacean dialects had been translated. A newcomer could spend his time listening to the glorious oral epics of the sulphur-bottom whale. Many were adopted into pods. The wisdom of the great whales became their inheritance. It was no surprise to Y41-AK9 when the initial audit after the Awakening showed these amiable philosophers to be farther along the Path to Understanding. He was just an old shark fighter who knew how to survive.

The Sentinel has the Tropique's head in close-up focus during the critical phase of the operation. Y41-AK9 is not interested in the techniques of chemical surgery, but he pays close attention as the healer applies a cellular solvent to the exterior cranial surface. The liquid solvent is traced on human tissue with a needlepoint stylus. Against the bone white of the cranium, the fine blue line looks as innocuous as ink, yet the solvent takes effect in less than a minute. The healer gives a slight pull and the skull comes apart exactly along the line. Almost a pint of liquid drains out onto the ground.

The moment is come. The cranial container is opened and the healer reaches in with her hands (with her *hands!*) and withdraws the brain of Obu Itubi. Y41-AK9 is spellbound. It seems so simple. The brain is rinsed of electrolyte solution and held in place as the healer meticulously reconnects severed nerves, arteries, and veins with organic adhesive. Y41-AK9 feels the beginnings of an old regret. Obu Itubi is free! Free to walk the earth again, to be among men. And all because of luck, simple haphazard luck. The same damned luck that doomed him to a career of combat with hammerheads and makos while others were born to have a whale for a guru. But this time it is different. Itubi will not get away. Even if it takes a hundred years, the Auditor will triumph. This time the luck will be his.

Unlike Y41-AK9, Auditor Quarrels is not a mystic by nature. As a young man he was a hedonist, a playboy jet pilot tending a napalm rose garden. Sex and speed were his obsessions. A war in Southeast Asia provided ample amounts of both. The war happened to Quarrels at Mach II; it was totally silent and calm. Night raids were the most beautiful. Only once was it real: a SAM missile hurtling up at the speed of sound out of the green-and-brown abstraction below. His elaborate evasion tactics, a grim, desperate ballet, first taught him that you become a mystic when it isn't fun anymore.

The lure of glamour, movie-star girlfriends and the fastest playthings on earth attracted Quarrels to the space program. He got it all as an astronaut, along with space in the bargain. Quarrels never wanted to come back down. And so he volunteered for the Aldebaran Expedition.

The three-hundred-and-twenty-year voyage of *Endurance II* proved the spacecraft worthy of her name. For Quarrels it was a rite of passage, an initiation earning him a residency on Level II of the Depository. Quarrels is content being a cerebromorph. His body was old, worn-out. He left it gladly and didn't mourn when it burned along with the rest of North America in the Thirty-minute War.

Hardship and disappointment seemed meaningless when confronted by the vast eternal tranquillity of the cosmos. Suffering, regret, anguish, envy—all of the old woeful earth-bound pains were purged by the awesome grandeur of space. Since his return from the Aldebaran system nothing has disturbed the serenity of the only Level II resident not born in a hatchery. The destruction of Skeets Kalbfleischer's brain is a setback for Auditor Quarrels, but the Commission notes that he takes the news calmly and without emotion. Truly remarkable for a native of the most neurotic century the world has ever known.

And later, when the report comes from the Medical Authority, Quarrels loses none of his calm self-possession. There are no facilities available for the production of cerebral tissue; the hatcheries are not equipped to manufacture brains; the perfection of the modified (brainless) humanoid is the result of years of genetic research. Moreover, Center Control regulations forbid any departure from established procedure. Requisition denied.

Vera wakes with her head throbbing. She shuts her eyes to the brightness of the open window and drops back into a canyon of eiderdown pillows. Her pulse thunders between her temples like the muffled kettledrums of a funeral cortege. The headache sends tendrils of pain downward through her body. Her limbs are heavy and sore, her breasts swollen, eyelids puffed and tender. She hurts all over. Vera wishes the funeral were her own: the padded satin of the coffin, the numb nothingness of death, a tomb's cool enclosing silence.

On other mornings, Vera found her slender adolescent body marked by love bites and scratches. Often she identified the lover by his imprint on her flesh: the itching thorn scratches on her nipples, the delicate canine punctures of blue-ribboned Hugo. Vera learned about hickies in Hollywood, but the ripe raspberry memories of passionate kisses could have come from any of a hundred casual pickups among the film colony. How amusing to discover the traces of a middle-aged passion blemishing her flawless schoolgirl's complexion.

Today she is not amused. The pain is too great for any pleasure, the pulsing headache an agony she has long forgotten. Two teeth are loose and her jaws open only with difficulty. She recognizes the author of these discomforts. Her first husband was fond of beating up people. He would provoke arguments in restaurants just for the chance to use his fists. A brutal man. Vera had been first attracted as much by his savagery as by his hard athletic body. He was a hunter, the son of a French industrialist. He took Vera on expeditions to India and Africa and introduced her to the catharsis of the clean kill. (The tigerskin on the floor was a souvenir of a trip made with Raoul.) At night he would come for her with a riding crop, although she feared his heavy gold-ringed hands much more. He beat her until she couldn't stand, seeking submission, not pleasure, and when she was on her knees he took her from the rear like an animal.

She tried to hide from him, sleeping on couches and under the billiard table in the library, as he stalked through the dark château. One night he cornered her in the trophy room and she seized a shotgun from the wall rack and added another corpse to the collection. The mounted shadows of oryx, kudu, Grant's gazelle, and the world's record rhinoceros were the only witnesses. The police reluctantly accepted her sobbing story of burglars and mistaken identity. The publicity was a great boost for her career.

But this was centuries ago, at Montigny-sur-Ourcq with its medieval keep and crenelated battlements crouching under a sullen sky. Vera sits up with a groan and confronts the summer luminance of a Caribbean morning. She hasn't thought of Raoul since that night she pulled the trigger. All memory of her husband's cruelty was cleanly erased by a magnum goose load of number four shot. Why then should he haunt her on her secret island?

Vera eases out of bed and limps to the dressing table to examine Raoul's handiwork in her mirror. Raw wales and welts are everywhere on her body, even her stomach bears a painful stripe, but her face shows the worst damage. Through dark swollen eyes, Vera studies the ugly purple shine of her bruised cheeks and the bee-sting puffiness of a cut upper lip. She'll wear tinted sunglasses today and a wide-brimmed hat for the comfort of its concealing shadows.

Vera crosses the hall to the *guardarropa*, remembering a long-sleeved summer gown tucked in a trunk somewhere. Although there is no one to witness her wounds, there are many mirrors and Vera wants to look her best, if only for herself.

She is searching through a deep leather trunk for a scarf to match her dress when she makes an entirely different discovery: the side-by-side Holland & Holland twelve gauge, one of a matched pair Raoul had bought in London, the weapon her groping hand chanced to find on the gun rack in the darkness long ago. Vera stares at the shotgun for a moment: the sheen of the richly blued barrels, the hand-rubbed gloss of the walnut stock, remembering her moment of terror among the stuffed animals, antlers twisting like tree branches above her in the gloom.

For a joke, she brings the piece to her shoulder, sights down its length, and whispers, "Bang." Perhaps, she thinks, returning the shotgun to the trunk, that will kill the ghost who was so rough with me last night. She closes the lid and her wish comes true. Splattered against the opposite wall is the same gory pattern of stray pellets, bone shard, brains, scraps, hair, and tattered flesh that the police spent long hours photographing the morning after. An eyelid clings to the full-length mirror. Vera screams and runs from the room, skidding on the fragments of teeth scattered across the parquet floor.

Obu Itubi opens his eyes. A fierce blue sky curtains his nightmare visions and his terrified scream constricts into a gasp of amazement. The fear remains, a palpable demon lurking just behind the protective gauze of sun-bright clouds. For the moment anyway, he is safe. As long as his eyes are open, nothing can happen to him.

The realization that he has eyes and is not seeing the world through a scanner comes at the same moment he discovers his hands. Are these his hands? This face he feels, can it be his? Cheeks, nose, lips—Itubi pokes a thumb into his eyeball and laughs for joy at the tears and the sharp lingering pain. He looks up at the palms of his hands, a latticework of fingers dividing the sky, and delights in a barrage of sensation: hot sun on his skin, the smell of pinewoods, a soft tickling underneath him. He sits up laughing.

Three Nords stand and watch. Their embroidered costumes and bleached-wheat hair anchor them like monuments against a background of whirling green. There is too much to see: trees, grass, flowers; the whole earth around him a dizzying blur while these three splendid humans loom as distinct as giants.

"Welcome," one says, smiling, his voice loud and glad. "You are reborn."

Auditor Quarrels prepares a final Commission Memorandum on Subject Denton Kalbfleischer. Hoping to find evidence that his sexual therapy was at least in part beneficial, he submits Vera Mitlovic's file number to the communicator. Pre-programmed information is returned instantaneously: THE RESIDENT YOU WISH IS TEMPORARILY DISCONNECTED ON ALL CHANNELS.

This is annoying. Can Center Control still be enforcing disciplinary isolation? Quarrels decides to check it with Vera's Auditor, but when he signals on the Commission's special channel code he hooks up with the Denton at Aud-Com HQ instead.

THE AUDITOR YOU ARE SEEKING IS DISCONNECTED AND OFFICIALLY SANCTIONED FOR VOLUNTARY TRANCE RETREAT.

All right, when will he be returning?

THE TRANCE IS SCHEDULED FOR INDEFINITE DURATION.

I certainly wish him luck.

LUCK?

It is my wish that his endeavor prove enlightening.

THAT IS TO THE PURPOSE. LUCK IS NOT A FACTOR IN THE SYSTEM. THE LAWS OF CHANCE DO NOT APPLY IN THIS SITUATION.

Look, I'm not about to discuss semantics with you today. What is happening to this Auditor's caseload?

CENTER CONTROL REGULATION 24-092: ALL SUBJECTS HAVE BEEN ASSIGNED APPROVED STUDY PLANS AND ARE MONITORED BY COMMISSION HQ.

Thank you. I am familiar with the regulation. You have been most helpful. As always, the dependable Deltron.

THE SERIES IS PROUD OF ITS REPUTATION.

Rightly so, why shouldn't a machine be permitted the luxury of pride. End transmission.

In Philip Quarrels' opinion the Deltron is as dull a machine as the Amco-pak series, for all of its renowned dependability. And so sanctimonious about the Trance Retreat. To Quarrels, it is just another overambitious Auditor risking everything for a quantum jump to the Great Liberation. The last three levels in the System involve isolation and total withdrawal, and residents are known to have been elevated hundreds of degrees at one time, skipping all intermediary levels on the Path to Understanding. But an indefinite trance state is a gamble; most of those who take the chance come back babbling, candidates for emergency therapy.

Quarrels prefers the Path of Obedience and Dedication. At the moment, he has a memorandum to finish and an interview with Vera Mitlovic is essential. By regulation, Inter-level memory-merge is only permitted between an Auditor and his subject. Quarrels has often regretted not attempting such a merge with Skeets. The boy was a Scout; they could have gone on camping trips together, swapped yarns around a roaring fire, become pals. It is too late now for regrets; the best he can do for Skeets is file a complete memorandum.

Quarrels knows that if he wants to talk with Vera it will have to be on the island. Her cranial container is in isolation and he couldn't communicate without the entranced Auditor's authorization. Quarrels arranged Vera's merge with Skeets. He knows the correct coordinates; simple rewiring is all that is required. Even his background is right. As a young pilot, Quarrels was stationed at Boca Chica Naval Air Station and made frequent flights down through the Caribbean. Once he was forced to eject after a flame-out over Tortola.

Also, there's a sentimental coincidence in breaking regulations this one time. During the Apollo Project, when astronauts had considerable cachet as celebrities, Philip Quarrels was a familiar figure in Hollywood; movie studios often arranged dates for him with aspiring starlets and go-go girls. He received invitations to all the best parties. At one such poolside occasion he picked up a flashy European actress and spent a delirious weekend with her at a motel outside Palm

Springs. They never saw each other again, although he went to several of her pictures. Her name was Vera Mitlovic.

Y41-AK9 watches on his scanner. The Nords help Itubi to dress, outfitting him with extra garments from their pack-baskets. There is no talk after exchanging names. Itubi follows like a clumsy child and stands to one side, watching as the Nords prepare torches. The fire frightens him; a close-up of his eyes reveals utter panic as the pyre is ignited.

Communication channels are at last open to the surface installation. Y41-AK9 commands the lens and the Sentinel's movement, but when he orders the hovering robot to restrain the Tropique he gets no response. Man is sacrosanct to a machine; inhibitions are built in at the factory; the order is meaningless.

Itubi follows when the Nords start single file for the woods, leaving a gathering of maintenance vans to witness the end of the funeral pyre. The Sentinel is right behind, skimming over the tree tops. Y41-AK9 watches Itubi struggle to keep up, tripping on exposed roots and thrashing in the underbrush. The contrast with the Nord's agile grace amuses the Auditor. Every clumsy movement, each comic pratfall endorses the validity of the Depository System. Itubi's undignified performance is typical of a Level I resident. It takes more than a body to make a man.

Back in her bedroom, with the door locked, Vera regains composure by breathing deeply and concentrating on the frangipani tree outside the window. Her morning orange juice is untouched in a goblet beside the bed. She takes a calm and grateful sip. The flavor is strangely wrong. A hint of almonds recalls a deranged Norwegian wardrobe mistress who doused her snacks with cyanide for several months before she was exposed by the death agonies of a miniature schnauzer greedy enough to make off with a box of contaminated *marrons glacés.*

Vera spits the suspicious mouthful into a wash basin. First Raoul and now Hilda; the past grows malevolent. A beating is bad enough, but she has no intentions of spending half her days in bed with stomach cramps. Her original misgivings about the house seem justified; all that treacherous nostalgia. Memories grow musty like everything else. It is time for some fresh air.

In a field outside of town, Vera slips a halter over Chi-Chi's nose for the first time in what must be weeks. Her wide-brimmed sunhat makes a slow walk the only practical gait and the horse plods along the dusty road leading to the beach. A steady wind sends serpentine waves rippling across an ocean of sugarcane. She stares aloft at the motionless glide of a man-o'-war bird as an orange-and-white striped parachute opens like a flower against the distant blue of the sky.

Philip Quarrels watches the island enlarge between his feet, thinking: fifty years since the last drop, sealed in the scorched hull of all that remained of *Endurance II*. But it is a memory of something which has not happened to him yet, for this is the young pilot's first jump and he clings to the shrouds, so excited he is unable to keep from smiling at the prospect of thirty million dollars' worth of aircraft nosediving into the empty Atlantic.

An eight-knot wind carries him north northeast, across the island. Details on the ground emerge out of the patchwork geometry: a single-track dirt road dividing the even rows of cane, a circle of tapering royal palms surrounding an acre of scum-green pond, an abandoned greathouse, the shell of a ruined windmill, a girl on a horse. Suddenly, a tamarind tree expands beneath him like an opening umbrella. Quarrels hauls at the lines, fighting for every foot as he drifts past the threatening limbs and into the green uprush of a grass-covered hillside.

He is standing on the collapsed chute, unfastening his harness straps, when the girl comes riding over the crest of the hill. She stares at him, anonymous behind dark glasses and the shielding hatbrim. Her glossy black hair is tied in a single braid down her back like a schoolgirl, yet the dress she wears suggests sophistication and maturity in spite of the way the skirt is pulled up to expose her slim tanned legs. It is a dress designed for buffet garden luncheons and lounging on sofas in the late afternoon, and looks as out-of-place on horseback as does his Day-glo orange flight suit grounded in the relentless tropic sun.

"Hello, Vera."

"Who are you?"

"My name is . . . Quarrels, Philip Quarrels." He wonders if she remembers the Palm Court Motel.

"How do you know who I am?"

"I'm . . . a friend of Skeets'."

"Oh?" Vera laughs, not the nervous giggle of a young girl; the chill sound is bitter and sardonic. "Well, he's gone. You missed him."

"Yes, I know. There was an accident."

"What do I care about that?"

"He didn't suffer. It was instantaneous. I thought you'd like to know."

"You're from the Depository."

"Well . . . I—"

"Don't deny it, you didn't just drop out of the sky. What do you want with me?"

"Nothing definite."

"*Merde!* You wouldn't be here if you didn't want something. What is it? Did they send you to bring me back?"

"No, nothing like that, I don't think they even know you're here. I only want to talk for a little while."

"Talk? What about?"

"Skeets."

"*Skeets?*" The name is lost in cynical laughter. Vera clutches her flopping hat, drives her heels into the horse's flanks, and gallops out of sight over the hill.

Obu Itubi sits with his back against the rough bark of a lodgepole pine, limp as a stringless marionette. His legs ache, his face and arms are scratched and bruised, his blistered feet a throbbing reminder of the many miles he's come from the Depository. A host of other minor discomforts—itching insect bites, a sunburned nose, the prickling of dried sweat, the unfamiliar demands of thirst and hunger—all declare that the distance to Aisle B must be measured in something more than mere miles.

The three Nords set up camp. Skiri and Gregor gather firewood; Swann arranges the sleeping robes. They seem as fresh now as when Itubi followed them into the woods. No words are spoken; indeed, there has been no conversation all afternoon. Reticent Northerners, Itubi thinks, a group of Tropiques would have spent the day laughing and singing.

They are a cold people, it's in the blood. The woman is attractive, yet the men show no interest in her; thin sap runs in their veins. Itubi watches Swann bend over the packbaskets; the movement of her breasts under the woven tunic kindles an ancient longing. Here is no electric dream. Tired as he is he can still pleasure a woman, and fight to keep her, too, if those pale milksops should care to protest.

Swann senses his eyes upon her and looks up from her work. "You've had a long day," she says, moistening a cloth in the waterskin hanging heavily under a pine bough. "You should rest."

"Time enough for that," he says, as she wipes the grime from his face and cleans the cuts on his cheek.

"You'll soon grow used to the woods. Coordination will come and you won't get in the way of every swinging branch. Remember, your body is only an extension of the mind. Be alert."

Itubi disregards the sermon. "You must have a very beautiful mind," he says, reaching out to sift her fine blond hair through his fingers.

"Why do you say that?"

"Because you have such a lovely body." Itubi caresses her cheek and when she doesn't respond, he slips his hand behind her neck and starts to draw her down into an embrace. Swann smiles, calmly taking hold of his wrist.

"And you have a very rapid heartbeat," she says, feeling his pulse rate with her fingertips. "I suggest a good night's sleep."

The cold Nord bitch! A corpse has more fire and passion than this frigid nursemaid. It is no wonder the other men ignore her. Itubi is disgusted. At the same time he feels a glow of pride for his own Class: a Tropique wench would at least have slapped him. What an insipid lot these Northerners are.

Itubi's question is spontaneous: "How did you know I was a Tropique?"

"You are what you are. What you were no longer matters."

"But, how did you know? Why did you put me in a Tropique body?"

"I picked the first undamaged body that was available. It was just coincidence."

"You mean, I could have become a Nord?"

"As a matter of fact, we considered the body of a Nord female, but she had no legs."

"A Nord . . . female!"

"Would that have disturbed you so very much?"

Itubi is speechless. Swann places a hand on his forehead.

"You're running a slight fever. I forgot you're from the first level and probably still attached to your identity. I shouldn't trouble you."

"Doesn't it matter to you who you are?"

Swann smiles. "Now, yes, of course, but I have been reborn. Whoever I was in the Depository is dead now. You're alarmed because I might have been a man, or an Amphíbios, but such distinctions don't exist on the upper levels; compared to Liberation, how important are those slight differences of sex or class? The Depository maintains a constant population in the world; when there's a death, the vacancy is filled by a member of the corresponding class and sex. The first qualifying cerebromorph is chosen. A simple and efficient method. Life is what matters. I might just as easily have been given Gregor's body, or Skiri's. But I'm tiring you. This is your first day and you're exhausted. You should sleep. I'll prepare some medication for your fever."

While Swann mixes her powders, the men return with armloads of dry wood and soon have a fire started. Itubi watches them silently prepare the evening meal and wonders to what sort of world he has returned.

Vera is not surprised to see the stranger in the orange suit trudging up the bone-white beach. The island is small and Chi-Chi's tracks are easy to follow in the wind-smoothed sand. She gauged her distance carefully: far enough to express displeasure, but not too far to discourage an active search. As he approaches, she adjusts the hem of her skirt, exposing a few additional inches of sun-ripened thigh, and affects an air of indifference.

"Hello," he calls. "I'm sorry if I upset you a while ago. I thought you'd be anxious for some news."

Vera rises on her elbows to face him. "Please, no more about Skeets." Noticing his eyes upon her legs, she arches a golden knee for emphasis. "It's all in the past now."

"I promise." He kneels next to her in the sand and offers a hand of mature bananas. "I found them growing by the road. They're very sweet."

Vera takes a banana. "What about you?"

"Thanks, I've had plenty. They're for you."

Vera smiles, managing to seem at once ingenuous and seductive. She peels the banana with a knowing leer, removing the yellow skin strip by strip, like a courtesan exposing her lover's white flesh. Slowly, she takes the curving shaft of the fruit into her mouth, slipping the whole length past her lips' moist circumference and then withdrawing it by degrees, glistening with spittle, until only the tip remains between her teeth. Her eyes are languid and heavy lidded as she bites.

"Mmm, delicious," she mumbles.

Quarrels clears his throat. He seems unable to watch her rhapsodic chewing. "What happened to your face?" he asks, staring straight out to sea. "You're got some nasty bruises."

"I fell off my horse. Are you sure you don't want a banana?"

"Positive."

Vera studies the firm set of his jaw, the clean, angular profile. "I was hurt here too," she says, opening her dress to show a discolored shoulder and skillfully offering a pink glimpse of budding breast in the same gesture. Quarrels glances away quickly, intent on the breaking waves, and says something about the dangers of bareback riding. Vera finds even his clenched teeth attractive. She remembers a Grand Prix driver who wore her scarf for luck at Monte Carlo and an Oberleutnant in the SS who seemed too handsome to be truly her enemy. There were other men with the same look, men accustomed to risk and daring, precise, military, and yet, at the same time, free and independent. Living in a world of actors who made a career of imitating such virtues, Vera always found the real thing irresistible and was bedded by a pantheon of test pilots, Olympic skiers, racing drivers, big-game hunters, mountaineers, and, once, an American astronaut. They were all one man to her: a swashbuckling dream prince who courted women and danger with the same devil-may-care nonchalance.

A high-frequency electronic humming brings Vera out of her reverie. "What's that?" she demands.

"My wrist alarm," Quarrels says, rising to his feet. "I'm on auto-merge control and prescheduled for disconnection in sixty seconds. That was my warning."

"I don't understand."

"There isn't time to explain. I have to leave now. It'll be easier for you if you don't look. Less traumatic."

"Are you coming back?"

"I don't know. . . . It's against regulations."

"Please. I'll tell you anything you want to know about Skeets. Anything at all. Only promise to come back."

"Goodbye, Vera."

"I'm sorry I acted so stupidly."

"Don't apologize. I must go now."

"Next time I swear it will be different."

"Goodbye."

Quarrels turns and sprints up the beach. Vera watches the bright orange suit as he hurries around low clumps of sea-grape and coco plum trees.

"*Wait!*" Vera scrambles through the hot sand, holding her dress above her knees. "Don't go." She runs after him, past the bushes at the edge of the beach, and into a grassy shaded grove of coconut palms. "*Phil!*" She stops, searching the green expanse for even a trace of his Day-glo costume.

Except for Chi-Chi, grazing peacefully a hundred yards away, the grove is deserted.

Devotion to duty is the goal of Level II and an Auditor's busy schedule leaves little time for leisure. As much as Y41-AK9 would like to personally conduct the surveillance of subject Obu Itubi, his crowded agenda makes this impossible. Other duties require his constant attention and he assigns a clerical machine at AudCom HQ to monitor the Sentinel's scanner signal and edit those portions not of immediate interest. The silent hours of sleep are of no concern, and whole days of hiking without a single word exchanged are erased by the Magnacor-650, along with the nightly repetition of camp-site chores. At the end of a week, the file programmed for Y41-AK9 is less than ten minutes long. There are three episodes on the brief file.

The first occurs on the bank of a mountain lake. It is late afternoon, calm and silent; no breeze disturbs the mirror-still surface and, except for the dimpling rise of occasional trout, there is little to distinguish the placid water from the cloud-flecked sky above. Obu Itubi lies full length on the trunk of a pine fallen out over the lake. He rigs a trotline, tying the end to an upright branch, and while the others gather firewood, he waits face down on the mossy log, staring at his reflection in the water.

The file cuts to early morning. Following a game trail, the party passes within a dozen meters of a salt lick. Itubi points at two strangers, both Nords, standing immobile under the trees. Skiri and the others act unconcerned.

"But, what's the matter with them?" Itubi asks. "They seem to be in a trance."

"Hunters," Skiri tells him. "I fear we have prolonged their wait."

"Hunters? I thought you people didn't eat meat."

"We don't. The nuts and cereals and dried fruit we share with you are our only diet. These hunters look for illness and disease. When they find an animal that might infect others, they destroy it painlessly. The meat is left as carrion, but we use the hide and bones. A trance state enables them to leave their conscious minds and wait for days without moving if necessary, silent and free from thought. Animals approach without fear."

The Sentinel's long-distance lens clearly catches the incredulity on Itubi's face.

Later, they encounter an old man, sitting alone in the lotus pose at the center of a small clearing. Like the hunters, he is naked. He smiles as they pass, but makes no other sign of greeting. Swann, Gregor, and Skiri each bow respectfully and avert their faces, but Itubi looks the old Nord straight in the eye. Except for his thinning hair and the fine network of incised wrinkles, he appears no older than Skiri.

"What's that one hunting," Itubi asks once they are back in the shadow of the woods. "Butterflies?"

"Your sarcasm is inappropriate, Obu," Swann says. "He is waiting for death."

Secure in the monastic confines of his cranial container, Philip Quarrels contemplates the pernicious nature of his desire. It is bad enough that a resident of Level II, a Class C Auditor, should be suffering the pangs of lust, but what makes the whole affair monstrous is that the object of his libidinous yearnings is only a child.

Quarrels' attempts to reconcile his memories of the Hollywood Vera (all paint and peroxide, a caricature voluptuary) with the slim dark-haired girl who sat beside him on the beach are no help. The thought of that faraway Palm Springs weekend only intensifies his longing.

The girl's eyes were his undoing. He was able to ignore her adolescent flirting, the enticements of her nubile teenage body, but when she removed her sunglasses to plead for his return he was lost. For a moment he didn't comprehend. Her innocent, bruised face was so deceptively vulnerable that it took him several seconds to notice the violet eyes glowering under those swollen discolored lids: the most depraved he had ever seen in his life.

Quarrels knows he should seek help before it is too late. He should report the whole business to his Auditor, confess his unnatural attraction to the delicate girl whose saintly face frames a sadist's eyes. He is so close to Elevation that it is a shame to spoil his chances by surrendering to secret passion. Instead, he reviews his schedule to determine when he will have enough free time to squeeze in another brief merge. Just one more time, he assures himself. This next will be the last. It is in the interest of self-knowledge. There can be no real harm in that.

After the noon meal, Obu Itubi wanders with his friends around the outskirts of the Nord village. This settlement of the Xi tribe contains only one permanent structure, a hand-hewn log-walled lodge rising to tree top height among the pines on the shore of the lake. Inside the great hall, with its overhanging balconies and broad staircases, are dormitories where the tribe lives communally after the snows come. For warmth, steaming water from a nearby hot spring is diverted into a network of ceramic pipes laid under the floor planking. Even in mild weather, when most of the Xi Nords live outdoors in tents and on platforms built high in the trees, the tribe takes all meals together inside, on long trestle tables gathered around the circular stone hearth in the center of the hall.

Itubi learns these facts from Skiri, who visited the Xi tribe on Quest twenty years before. The Navigator shows him the village, answering his many questions with a tolerant smile. Among themselves, the Nords seldom speak and Itubi is certain they practice some form of telepathy. How else can they anticipate one another so unerringly? A day's march ends without discussion; camp chores are never assigned; decisions come without words. If they are not actual mind readers, then how explain lives so attuned and harmonious? Telepathy might be rationalized as a trick, a freak of nature. But to accept the evidence of their Enlightenment, their seeming *prajna*. . . .

Itubi refuses to believe his companions are really any different from himself. In time, he'll grow used to the world again. He's been away for a long time. Things may have changed, but he'll soon catch up. And yet, Itubi is uneasy when he remembers the unearthly grace of the Nords. In a score of days, he never once saw Swann or Skiri or Gregor make a clumsy move. They seem free from all the little accidents to which he is prone: cutting his fingers, stubbing his toes, burning his mouth on hot food. They never trip or stumble or grow tired on the trail. Whenever the party stopped it was always at Itubi's request, and yet they each carried a heavy packbasket and his only load was the clothing he wore. Some mornings they rested a dozen times on his account, never complaining or showing anger. Nothing disturbs their eternal calm. The same placid smile remains on their lips. They are always at peace.

A similar peace prevails in the Xi village. Itubi hears the sounds of men at work: a blacksmith hammering at his forge, carpenters repairing the shake-shingle roof of the lodge, the steady scrape of a cooper shaping barrel-staves with a spokeshave. But something more important is missing: there are no children in the village. Instead of the laughter and shouting of children's games, the familiar wail of babies, there is only the high solitary quaver of a reed flute lost among the pines.

Itubi follows the path down toward the lake, listening to the unseen musician. Off to his left, a funeral pyre is prepared for the old man they passed yesterday in the woods. In another day or so, a party will search for his body. Swann explains the custom. The old go off alone when it is time to die.

"Why can't the hatcheries supply the aged with new bodies?" Itubi asks.

Swann only smiles.

"Death is the natural consequence of life," Skiri says. "For the reborn it is an end to Illusion."

Along the shores of the lake the Nords mend their nets while others carve and paint the goose decoys. The Xi tribe are down gatherers. In the season when the aspen changes color, great flocks of geese migrate from the north. The decoys are arranged on the lake and the fierce honking birds are trapped in nets dropped from the trees as they land. After the down is plucked from under the contour feathers on their breasts, the geese are released, alive and unharmed. Skiri explains the importance of this village. "The down for the winter clothes of Northern people all over the world is gathered here. This is the only source. That is why the Xi village is so large."

"Large?" Itubi laughs.

"Yes, this tribe numbers almost five hundred, one of the biggest on the continent. Only groups which perform a necessary function, like down gathering, cotton growing, or salt mining, need be so large. They labor for the common good. Most of the nomads—like the Omega, my own tribe, or the Lambda, who follow the caribou, or the Omicron, who tend the sheep herds—are quite small in number. Many do not live in tribes at all. It is not required. There are many solitary hunters. And, of course, those who are on Quest."

"But what about the cities?"

"There are no cities."

Itubi remembers Capetown, Nairobi, Dakar, and Rio, the great metropolitan centers of his age, glittering edifices of steel and glass towering under mile-high domes, monorails, moving sidewalks, hanging gardens, completely air-conditioned and computer controlled. Cities were the wonder of the earth. "No cities?" he murmurs in disbelief.

"The last cities were razed when the Depository was built. The metal they contained was stockpiled and should last for countless eons."

"The cities I knew were not built to be scrapheaps," Itubi says. "They were works of art."

"Art?" Skiri raises an eyebrow. "What do you mean by art?"

Itubi loses his temper. "Art," he yells, "sculpture, painting, music, literature, architecture . . . *art!*"

"The indulgent excess of the Ego, a feeble grasp at immortality. Little of what you call art remains. There is music, of course, to elevate the spirit, and a few of the ancient buildings survive. Temples, cathedrals, holy places that celebrate the All-in-One."

Itubi feels the weight of a great depression. Life seems as hopeless and futile as in the Depository.

"Then what is it all for?" he asks. "Is man only good for grubbing in the dirt or hunting with spears like savages? What's the purpose? Why does man even need to exist?"

Skiri's answer is calm and deliberate. "We are the Guardians."

"And that's all?"

"That is everything. The world is ours to preserve. We are the Guardians."

5. Larva

WITH POWER BACK to normal in the subdistrict and the
period of emergency operations at an end, many Level I residents find they are no longer satisfied with life as it was. The
possibility of actual danger has increased their expectations
and the prospect of endless anticipatory days at the scanner
appalls even the most dedicated viewer. For the first time in
centuries, the comic clumsiness of that perennial favorite,
the Amco-pak series, fails to draw an appreciable audience.

As the ennui spreads, so does the legend of Obu Itubi. The
official report of a malfunctioning Mark X is disregarded by
all but the most gullible in the System. Those who scanned
the flight are besieged with thousands of requests for details.
One scanner witness has become famous because he thought
to make a memo file of the battle between the maintenance
vans. Copies are circulated throughout the subdistrict via
communicator. Print quality is a good indication of one's

social standing; each retransmission blurs the image. Those without status must be satisfied with grainy files resembling twentieth-century color TV reception. There is a certain irony in that many of these same residents spent much of their time on their backsides guzzling beer in front of the flickering tube back in the days when there still were backsides and beer, and gullets to guzzle it with.

The beach is less than a hundred meters long, a pink parabola of coral sand protected at either end by jagged rock walls. Black and moon-pocked with sharp-edged craters where Triassic gas bubbles burst on the surface of a molten river, the violent contorted shapes threaten the tranquillity of the water and the palm-shaded carpet of deep pangola grass above the beach.

Vera lives in a billowing tent made from the parachute the mysterious Mr. Quarrels left behind. She has a splendid view of the sea and, off to one side, a waterfall streams from the rocks into a deep crystal pool overgrown with lime trees and sugar apple. There is an abundance of other fruit within a few kilometers of the tent. Vera gathers mangoes, guavas, bananas, soursop, avocados, and papayas in the lush, green forest.

For whatever else she requires, Vera makes frequent trips back to the house, raiding the pantry and the wine cellar. She takes what she can carry, piling the patient Chi-Chi like a peddler's nag. After the first week, she has supplied her secluded cove with the comforts of a sultan. Layers of Oriental rugs cover the tent floor; piles of silken cushions provide a bed; her tigerskin guards the door. There are mirrors, bowls and silver candelabra, chests of jewels and clothing. Chinese scrolls and woven tapestries hang in place of walls. The air is fragrant with sandalwood. Quarrels will have no trouble finding her; the bold orange-and-white stripes of his parachute are clearly visible through the shielding trees. Inside, Vera waits like a perfumed houri for the moment of his inevitable return.

With each passing day the river's changes grow more subtle. The first week's dramatic sequence of portages around cataracts and waterfalls and shooting white-water rapids through narrow sunless canyons has given way to broad meandering stretches. The canoe rides lightly as a drifting leaf on the rain-swollen current. Obu Itubi rests his paddle across the gunwales and studies the shore. Cottonwoods and willows grow along the bank. Beyond them the landscape is treeless, a rolling succession of grass-covered hills, empty as the sky. To Itubi, it seems a wasteland, barren and forbidding. In his time gardens were here, bountiful green farms evenly divided by irrigation canals and lovingly tended by automated agrocombines. These dedicated machines analyzed the soil, distributed organic nutrient, planted, destroyed harmful insects with high-frequency sound, harvested, plowed, and rotated the crops seasonally.

For a moment, Itubi can almost see the world as it was: domed crystal cities, powered by waste-free solar energy, isolated islands of civilization. Oz-like in their splendor, surrounded by an unending order of gardens, orchards, fields, canals, and rectangular lakes.

Itubi remembers a fertile mosaic of cultivation. The deserts bloomed. The oceans prospered. Man's benign influence was everywhere. Even the forests were tame and manicured. Unlike the barbaric wilderness between the Depository and the Xi village, the woods of Itubi's time were comfortable suburbs. In the twenty-second century, those who didn't care for cities or the undersea reef colonies lived in the rural mountains. Self-supporting plastic bubble homes, complete with computers, communication centers, recycling water, and individual solar energy accumulators were prefabricated and lowered into place from the air anywhere on earth. Foundations were unnecessary, for the bubble homes settled on stilts that bored deep into the ground and anchored firmly. Man's domain was total; homesites were available in the Amazon jungle and the remote fastness of the Himalayas. Even the polar ice caps were settled by intrepid lovers of winter sports. The world Itubi has returned to seems a poor contrast with the one he left behind.

This interminably tedious canoe voyage, three weeks on

the river and no end in sight, would have been an easy matter of an afternoon's trip in the sleek gyro-gravcraft of Itubi's
day. Obu glances ruefully up at the persistent Sentinel hovering above the river, a taunting anachronism in this new savage land, and thinks of hurtling through the clouds. In the
Depository, the damn canoe trip would be a memory-file and
when it became unpleasant he could program a new Index
number and be instantly transported to a speeding gyro-
gravcraft or a spaceship or the wings of a gliding hawk.

The sound of Skiri's steady paddling brings Itubi out of his
reverie. The Navigator never mentions Itubi's idleness, but
his silent continuing efforts harbor an unspoken reproach.
Obu begins paddling again. In the weeks on the river his
hands have hardened and his arms and shoulders are brown
and strong. He has grown used to Skiri's silent ways. It
wouldn't surprise him to wake one morning and find the
Nord had disappeared in the night. That was how Swann had
gone, without a word of farewell. She vanished from the Xi
village and Itubi never asked the one question that troubles
him still.

Skiri claims a vision of sickness among their people came
to Swann in a dream—the Omegas and the buffalo alike rav-
aged by a mysterious pestilence—and that she left the Xi
encampment before daybreak. How Skiri knows about the
dream is not explained to Itubi.

Typical Nord mumbo-jumbo, like the way Gregor hesitated at the last moment and took his pack out of the canoe, remaining behind with the Xi people as Obu and Skiri started off down the river. Perhaps that was the goal to his Quest after all. Itubi doesn't care. None of it matters to him. All he wants is to return to his own kind, to be among Tropiques again. And if that means submitting to the mystic vagaries of the Nord mentality, so be it. If he could fool Center Control all those years, he can easily play the same game with Skiri for another few weeks.

Philip Quarrels stalls his return to the land of memory-merge make-believe with several weeks of deliberate busy work: reports, memoranda, analysis records, all the trivial minutiae available to an Auditor anxious to kill time. But procrastination in the name of abstinence is no virtue and he makes his arrangements accordingly, attending to last-minute business, adjusting the auto-merge control for a prescheduled disconnection, and hooking up to the coordinates which send him spinning down the electronic rabbit-hole to this shared seaside daydream.

He kneels in the damp earth and parts a protecting screen of ferns. Below, on the glistening beach, done to a turn with sunshine and basted in her own sweet sweat, Vera Mitlovic lies naked on her back, her ebony hair spread like a blanket beneath her. Quarrels sucks in his breath, a sigh in reverse. What is he doing on this imaginary island, he wonders, his scrotum tight with desire for the girlhood ghost of a casual pickup several lifetimes away?

His delusion is that he controls his destiny. He assures himself that he has come to further his self-awareness. Playing peeping tom is in no way detrimental if the keyhole provides a glimpse into one's own soul. Quarrels interprets his lecherous ogling as nothing more than creative meditation.

Vera rises to her feet and brushes the sand from her flanks as she heads for the sea. Quarrels delights in her girlish grace as she plunges through the surf, emerging reborn, like Aphrodite from the foam. Shining with sea water, she seems more than mortal: her young breasts, dew-bright rosebuds; her damp hair, a trail of midnight across her tawny skin; her madonna's face an innocent mask hiding the depravity in her amethyst eyes.

Quarrels' rapt gaze follows her across the beach, his deliberate breathing an effort to control the urgent tomtom throb of his orbiting heartbeat. He watches as she wades into the freshwater pool and rinses the salt from her hair under the waterfall. A towel hangs spiked on the thorns of a lime tree. Vera pats and dries her body, wrapping her wet hair in a terrycloth turban as she steps inside the undulant tent.

Quarrels fidgets among the ferns, reminding himself that this is only a dream. His youth, the hot tropic sun, the dazzling sea, the apparition housed under his circus-colored parachute—none of it is real. It is an imaginary Quarrels who strides manfully down the hillside and across the knee-deep pangola grass. His tumescence is but a figment of his computerized fancy. It's all a matter of connections and coordinates. Somewhere, in another universe, a cerebromorph is dreaming an electronic dream, a fantasy of an island paradise where a beautiful sea nymph reclines naked on a pile of silken cushions, waiting for the handsome navy pilot who lifts the diaphanous flap of her tent and enters with a smile.

After the second rehearsal, the machines assemble for final instructions. Playbacks of the run-through are programmed into the Amco-paks; the precision choreography of pursuit and destruction will be duplicated on schedule. Fifteen scanners are positioned along the aisle to record the event from all possible angles. A Mark V checks the setting for undetected flaws. The verisimilitude must be exact.

The Unistat 4000 in charge of the production calls for silence and positions the maintenance vans for the drama. Signals are given. A single tripped switch efficiently supplants the histrionic "lights, camera, action" of yesteryear, and the waiting Mark X speeds off down the aisle in imitation of desperate flight. A pair of Mark IXs follow right behind the dedicated pursuers. Two more vans appear at intersecting side aisles, blocking the last avenues of escape. The Mark X is trapped. The aisle is a cul-de-sac. A mammoth energy transmitter obstructs the far end, its complex facade bristling with exposed wires and conductors. A warning buzzer sounds; the words KEEP AWAY — HIGH VOLTAGE light up the faceplate with a lurid neon glare. The posse of Mark XIs slows to half speed but the runaway Amco-pak barrels straight ahead on a kamikaze collision course and, with five scanners watching, crashes into the transmitter and explodes in a nova burst of incandescent fire.

An instant replay satisfies the Unistat and prerecorded narration is added to the scanner file before it is dispatched to the Level I memory bank, the official Center Control report on the massive power overload that caused the recent emergency. Edited portions of the file are spliced into the memory-bank biography of resident Obu Itubi. Investigation of the wreckage reveals a critical short circuit in the Compacturon DT9 unit of the runaway Mark X. The captive resident was a powerless passenger aboard the berserk machine. In recognition of this tragic death, Center Control has ordered that the new automatic shut-off switch, recently installed in every member of the Amco-pak series, be named the Itubi Mechanism in his honor.

"Have I pleased you?" Vera whispers, her warm breath fanning Quarrels' cheek. There is nothing in her manner of the insecure adolescent seeking praise. Instead, the tone is haughty, her words rhetorical. She toys with a tuft of hair in his armpit. "Are you happy with me?" she asks, disinterested as a waiter inquiring about the wine.

Quarrels lies on his back, unable to answer. His abattoir eyes vacant and glazed, like a heifer's after the sledgehammer falls. He stares at the rippling parachute above his head, anchored by numb exhaustion. Is this happiness? This stunned desolate inertia? Can this be pleasure? Ensnared by lassitude, Quarrels regards the fire of his recent passion with detachment and disbelief. He wonders if his youth was ever so possessed and pities this driven mortal creature not yet purged by space.

"Don't look so sad," Vera scolds, massaging his chest with slender fingers.

"Am I being sad?"

"Such a long unhappy face."

"I don't feel sad. Perplexed maybe."

"Is it because of me that you're glum?"

"Sometimes even pleasant memories are painful."

"Then it's time for more pleasure." Vera siphons his nipple into the rolled tip of her tongue.

Quarrels regards the sleek child squirming in his arms. It seems impossible that so innocent a sylph initiates attitudes and techniques unfamiliar even to the mature Vera of his motel memories. Back in those Smilin' Jack days, Quarrels favored the double-entendres of his profession and made frequent conversational allusion to "joy-sticks," "cockpits," and "bailing out." This flight-deck humor was consistent with his reputation as an ace of the boudoir, but it served to cover up sexual adventuring as conventional as the manual of arms. For all his many conquests, Captain Quarrels has never encountered anyone to equal the teenage doxy who nibbles at his fingertips and blows saliva bubbles into his ear. Not even the CO's nymphomaniacal wife at Pensacola had been so inexhaustably acrobatic. None of the Saigon prostitutes were capable of such calculated innovation as Vera's trick of inserting a knotted silk scarf into his rectum (first lubricating the way with her ingenious tongue) and reaching behind as she rides him like a piston-powered jockey to remove it, one knot at a time, at the onset of his climax.

Vera's hands are busy, exploring thighs and stomach. She tends his flaccid cock as devotedly as a battlefield nurse caring for a fallen trooper. She cleans it with little catlicks, blowing gently where the skin is chafed. Quarrels marvels at the girl's magic. She is breathing life back into his loins. Incredibly, he wants her yet another time. He arches his back to receive the knotted scarf and the dream ends with the shrill complaint of his electric wrist alarm.

AudCom HQ signals when the weekly surveillance file is available and Auditor Y41-AK9 disconnects a lecture by Sri Aurobindo, regretfully turning his attention from the compassionate words of a great teacher to the vagabond behavior of his ego-ridden runaway subject. This river voyage is becoming as tedious for the Auditor as it is for Itubi.

In the white water there was hope for a capsized canoe

and subsequent remote control capture via Sentinel. (The machine's instructions would call it a rescue operation.) But the last two files show the river widening into an even mud-colored avenue, deep and fast-moving, a kilometer across to the opposing banks. The dugout sweeps along with only the random possibility of underwater snags.

This week's file begins: a high-altitude view of the delta, a broad alluvial fan spreading into the gulf, latticed by irregular channels and interconnecting creeks. The Sentinel holds, unseen, more than a myriameter above the curving coastline. A cut to a three-masted sailing ship over on its beam ends at low tide. Itubi and the Nord mingle with the crew gathered on the mud flat. A stranger paddles off in their canoe. Soon, he is lost among the bayous.

Y41-AK9 pays little attention to Itubi. His subject has signed up for a sea voyage. Nothing can prevent the tide from rising. Just as the file will end. Soon. Much too soon. For Y41-AK9 is entranced with the image of the master mariner, the first Amphíbios he has seen outside the Depository. The sun gleams on the smooth silver-blue skin and for a moment when he lifts his gaze, the Auditor can look into his multi-colored eyes and watch the rings of red, green, and black change and shift as the translucent inner lids slide into place.

Through the silken folds of the tent Vera watches her lover as he walks toward the beach. His buttocks are lean and small, tense muscles shift under the pale flesh with every step. Vera likes the way he moves.

He crosses the beach, hands on his hips, walking to the water's edge where the sand is wet and hard. He never waves or turns his head. Vera watches, careful not to blink, once it starts. First, there is a hint of color, a nacreous shimmer vibrating along his arms and back. For an instant, an iridescent chrysalis surrounds his body. The light intensifies. A quick flash and Phil Quarrels is gone, leaving a green blur hovering in Vera's retina, an optical ghost bisected by the line where the sea meets the sky.

She smiles, stretching her feet into the soft sand under the rug. She is pleased with herself. This time there was no pleading with Quarrels to stay. There wasn't the embarrassment of clinging to his legs. She knows she will see him again. When the wrist alarm sounded, she rolled easily from his arms and said, "Too bad you have to go. It spoils my surprise."

"What surprise?"

"Oh, I wanted to show you the diary I kept while Skeets was here. We would have a good laugh together."

Itubi skulks among the hawsers coiled in the bow. Not even the other Tropique crew members take his side in disputes with the vessel's master. They grovel and toady like a pack of pasty Nords, speaking in whispers, never raising their heads from work to join in songs or joke, not a word of

protest while that damn *tadpole* struts in his gossamer robes
and looks on when there's a yard to be hauled or a sail reefed.
Master mariner be damned, he was nothing but a fisheyed
tadpole to Itubi, a pompous cold-blooded tad.

Obu is glad the ship is not bound for Africa. Think of
months on the open sea, ruled by that reptilian, and for
what? He has no desire to see mangoes thrive where once
mighty Lagos towered. What value is the Benin heritage in a
world without art? Southern Hemisphere One doesn't sound
like home. Where he goes is not important. Any place will be
a beginning. The options are endless for the reborn.

Skiri told of islands lying ahead, a new landfall every few
days. It's a fine thing for the Navigator to meander about the
ocean on his Quest. His is an easy birth. Life on deck is not
so sweet. Another week at most is Skiri's guess, before the
green mountains rise out of the sea. A few more days of
drudgery. Itubi plans a campaign of Nordic piety: attentive to
his duties, tolerant of the master, indistinguishable from the
other toadies. No one will suspect his intentions until he is
over the side and away.

Becalmed. A fierce sun rages above the slackened sails. The
decks are spread with brightly woven carpets; hammocks
hang between the shrouds; a drum-taut tarpaulin rigged to an
idle spar shadows the six crew members. Itubi carves a bit of
hardwood salvaged from the northern forest. The keen cut-

ting blade is Gregor's gift. One of the Nords studies a painted scroll; the other strums a drone harp. Skiri works with his charts spread out on the patterned rug. Beside him, a Tropique hums the holy *AUM*.

The master mariner stands at the rail, his cobweb gown spilling like smoke from his shoulders. Spider silk provides the finest test for a weaver's fingers. It is the only fabric an Amphíbios can wear. Even the loose-fitting cotton tunic favored by Tropiques and Nords alike in hot weather will foul in the gill vents. Beneath the surface, there is no need for the constricting garments which shield his sensitive skin from the sun.

A form appears in the opalescent water. And another. Two bottle-nosed dolphins rise toward the hull and veer away, a single fluke slicing into the air. For a brief moment of recognition, the master mariner looks into a squinting eye. A cluster of froth marks their swift turn.

The master mariner loosens a clasp and his ephemeral garment slips to his feet. He climbs to the taffrail, the clefts of his gill intake showing under his arm as he reaches for the ratlines. His dive cuts the water with a soundless splash. A trail of bubbles marks his descent as he voids the terminal air in his lungs. Rising from the depths, he hears the silver oscillation of the dolphin's song.

Y41-AK9 ends an audit session with these words of advice for a lower-level subject:

You must relax. Without withdrawal from tension there can be no concentration. Tomorrow, during the meditation exercise, tune your mind to the alpha-wave broadcast; hear the sacred AUM, the shining sun of suns. Just as you have shed your physical body, be aware of the subtle nature of your astral body. Remember the nineteen elements which compose it: ten organs of action and knowledge, the five vital airs, plus the four mental principles, mind, intellect, subconscious, and ego. These all are shed at the moment of Liberation; the Great At-Oneness.

Find the Divine Power within you. Activate this manifestation of the universe; it is Serpent Power. Let the power uncoil, moving upward toward the seat of the thousand-petaled lotus in the brain. This is the union with pure consciousness.

End transmission.

AUM.

"Why go back?"

"The more serious question," Quarrels says, his eyes fixed on the sunset, "is why do I want to stay?"

"It's a good thing you're so sexy, you certainly win no points for flattery."

"Stop playing games, Vera. I'm not talking about passion, or that fascinating diary which keeps you so busy between my visits. I do like your pout, but that's not what's bringing me back. Each time I set the controls for a longer stay."

"Fuck the controls. This is as good as life has been in a long time and you know it. Admit it. Even for a fancy Level II Auditor, or whatever the hell you are, this is the best you can remember."

"How did you know I was from Level II?"

"Because you sound like a young abbé who once gave me music lessons, full of zeal and chastity. Quite good-looking, too. When were you cerebrectomized?"

"August 19, 1972." An easy date for Quarrels to invent. His thirty-second birthday, the day he stepped from the LMV to the surface of the moon.

"Seventy-two. That *was* early. You must have really been some kind of nut."

"No, it . . ." Quarrels gropes for another lie, "it was in Southeast Asia. I caught some junk on a strike. The navy picked up the pieces."

"Then you don't remember the pollution or the war? How life used to be, the air-conditioning and the gas masks? Oh, I had a charming mask from Gucci, all in python with a lot of style, but most people looked like insects on the street. The radiation suits were worse! Much too bulky to have any chic."

"I was spared that, thank God." This is true. From the orbiting space platform, the earth was a shining blue disk, only slightly smudged around the continents; and when the Thirty-minute War consumed half the globe, *Endurance II* was out beyond Pluto, seventy years deep into space.

"Well, my sheltered innocent, the world wasn't the pretty place you remember from before the middle war. By the time I went into the box, there were quite a few changes. Nothing as nice as this was left. You ought to stick around; there isn't a file in the Depository that can compare with life here. Who knows, if you stay you might find another airplane hiding someplace."

The Sentinel stands in a clearing shaded by mango trees circled by a dozen seated members of the only tribe on Antilles Nine, the Qaf. Because the tribe is symbiotic—Tropiques on the island and Amphíbios in the coral reef surrounding it—there are two Law Speakers. They stand on either side of the tall tripodal cylinder, listening with folded arms to the communicator voice of Y41-AK9:

You must understand that Level I is a refuse heap. No resident of Level I has ever been Elevated, nor is there a likely candidate among their numbers. They are thousands of years from even the beginnings of spiritual awakening. This runaway must be returned to the Depository. He has not earned the right to live among you.

"It is in his karma to be with us," the Amphíbios Law Speaker says.

True, Enlightened One, but his presence is a danger to your society. His unstable behavior makes harmonious life impossible. I am more convinced of this than ever after he deserted his shipmates and managed to elude observation for such a long time. Remember the destruction he caused in the Surface Installation.

"Only machines were destroyed," says the Tropique.

And the brain of a Level I resident.

"A brain is an organic machine, as replaceable as any other. Are the resident's files intact?"

To my knowledge, they are.

"Then, don't worry about the hardware. Develop some priorities."

"Perhaps," the Amphíbios says, covering his gleaming skull-bald head with a fold of his gown, "our worthy Auditor should not trouble himself with such refuse. Perhaps such matters do not concern his exalted attentions."

My words were ill chosen, Seer of Truth. Devotion to my subjects on Level I is my sacred duty.

"Just so."

Exactly why I must plead for the return of Obu Itubi.

The Tropique shakes his head. "It would be better if you examined your own motives. You might find your eagerness is caused by the demands of Ego. Obu is content here. Give him time to sort out his thoughts. He lives alone in a simple shelter built with his own hands. He's planted a garden. Such is the foundation of a full life."

A foundation built upon the sand will topple. I have had Itubi under continual surveillance since yesterday morning.

Are the Law Speakers aware that it's not a garden he tends, but a crock of fermenting guavas? Does the brewing of intoxicants yield a full life?

"A man's life is his own if he causes no harm to others."

With the Speaker's permission, I have preserved his words on memo file. There may be a time when he will want to hear them once again. Until then, I maintain Sentinel surveillance as authorized by Center Control.

"Peace be unto you and all living creatures."

Oona the Weaver wanders far into the backcountry each afternoon, hunting insects, plants, and other dye-stuffs under the arching canopy of trees. She carries a fiber basket for her cuttings and a pair of drawstring pouches to hold her more elusive discoveries. A dry streambed provides an easy pathway through the liana vines.

It is a warm flower-scented afternoon; slanting shafts of sunlight pierce the leaves and branches overhead; the only sound is a murmuring call of doves. Oona moves silently over the water-smooth stones. She feels the life energies of other creatures around her in the dense forest: young deer in velvet, sly mongooses on the prowl, lizards with their throbbing orange throats. She is aware, too, of another presence, vaguely dangerous like a sleeping snake. But, unlike the serpent's lethal torpor, the vibrations she senses from the hermit hidden in the underbrush are alive and desperate.

Obu Itubi watches the graceful hips and slender brown ankles; he notes the firm swell of her breasts under the white cotton shirt. This woman balancing a basket is a daily enticement, her invasion of his numb retreat a painful reminder of an old dream gone sour. Itubi takes a slobbering drink from his calabash. Belching bittersweet, he wipes his mouth on his forearm and smiles. Drunkenness helps to erase memory for a time. The pious hospitality of the Qaf Tropiques supplies his brewpot with honey as well as the bread he uses to start the mash working. Pure spring water and acres of fruit come free in the forest. He wallows in the sunshine, sodden and heavy with beer, indifferent to his misery until the woman comes every afternoon and makes him think of how it might have been.

She remains a stranger. He has never spoken or shown himself to her. He knows all too well the distant sound of her voice, the placid smile. Tropiques, Nords, men or women, they are all stamped from the same mold. Center Control adjusts the light that burns in the clear unwavering eyes. The outside world is only another level in the Depository System.

Still, it's fun to imagine stripping those floppy pajamas from her perfect shoulders, seizing breasts, hips, a fold of thigh, before plunging his face into the syrupy mussel-colored maw of her, to drink and taste, uncoiling his long tongue like a butterfly sipping nectar from a flower.

Nothing ever changes. Years seem to pass between Philip Quarrels' visits, and yet Vera detects no aging in her mirror. Time slips by, one day exactly like the next, yesterday the twin of tomorrow, and her only real memories are of the hours she spends with Philip. Even the house stays the same. When she returns for supplies this week (or was it last week, or last month?), the familiar sun-filled rooms seem as fresh and new as the day of her first visit.

She hurries through the pantry, filling her hamper with cheeses and tinned delicacies. Freshly baked bread and a tantalizing assortment of glacéd cakes wait in the kitchen. A trip to the wine cellar yields a half dozen dusty bottles. Vera dumps the trash she brings from her tent into a barrel in the yard outside the kitchen door. The barrel is empty as it will be next time, as it was the time before. And ever shall be, Vera thinks. Except when he's here. Then, it's almost real.

She lives in the shelter of his parachute, safe to borrow only those memories which are pleasant. Quarrels can never come to the house, she knows that too. Still, she wishes she could share some particle of her past with him. He is apathetic to the fine food and drink, sleeping as easily in the sand as in the nested pillows on her tigerskin. The treasures of her lifetime hold no interest for him. She wants something to please a man, something like Raoul's shotgun upstairs in the trunk.

The woman is on her knees in front of him, pulling tubers from the moist earth and placing them in her basket. At the sound of Itubi's lurching stumble she turns her head and starts to rise, but he catches her sleeve and pulls her down beside him in the leaves. He is a naked devil, tearing at her clothes, his florid face leering and wild. She lies inert, curious and detached as he parts her legs with a savage thrust of his knee.

Itubi sways, panting above her, his hands pinning her shoulders to the ground. "Too pure, aren't you?" he snarls as her eyes calmly meet his hate-filled stare. "Too pure and holy to fight back?" He slides his hands down to her breasts, cruelly pinching her nipples. "But you can't stop these from wrinkling and hurting and growing hard, can you?" She doesn't move. "What's the matter? Is your cunt so saintly? Is that what's the matter? The precious sepulcher is about to be defiled. Isn't that worth fighting for? Isn't it!"

"Your need is so great," Oona says, opening her thighs for him. "You must suffer." She slips her ankles behind his knees.

Itubi recoils, his hands lifting from her breasts as if the flesh has suddenly putrefied beneath his touch. "Oh no, I don't want that." He rises to his feet. "I'll do better with my fist, milking my dreams."

"But it's not for pity." Oona lifts her hand, fingers gently drifting along the silken shaft, tracing the swollen blood vessels like a blind woman. "I've seen does mounted in the forest and the copulation of whales, and every day in the barnyard the cock runs the hens to earth and I watch him cover them with his strong wings." She is standing beside him. "I am different from the others, like you are." She directs his fingers up between her legs. "The sight of a stag in rut never made me open in such a manner."

They cling together, moaning and swaying like trees in the wind. Uprooted, they fall back into the leaves. Itubi enters her with slow deep strokes and the spasms of release are immediate, all his tensions flooding helplessly into the soft enveloping warmth. For Oona it is something different. His passion is the threshold of an all-consuming universe, ever expanding into particles of light, the very atoms of her being disintegrate, electrons collide. She is lost in the electric fire of creation.

Spent, Itubi gamely endeavors to match Oona's voracious rhythm. He remains erect, but his mind is elsewhere. He is thinking of the drone bee mating in midair with the Queen, chosen out of a legion of pursuing bachelors. The nuptial flight ends in tragedy. The drone falls back to earth, disembowled, while the Queen flies off with his sexual apparatus and a portion of trailing abdomen still obediently pumping.

"Throw!"

Vera skims a flat-sided seashell up into the air, launching

it with a flick of her wrist like a tiny discus. Quarrels swings the shotgun in a sweeping arc, taking an extra second to gauge the lead. He fires and the seashell powders. Vera jumps up and down in the sand, applauding.

"You try," he says, slipping two red plastic cartridges into the smoking cylinders.

"No, it hurts my shoulder. I like throwing better."

"Can you throw two at once?"

"Why not?" She hunts along the surfline for shells the proper size. "Philip," she remembers to call him Philip, "isn't this fun, Philip?"

"Terrific." He grins.

"I hope it never ends."

"I'm going back to the Depository, if that's what you mean."

"Oh?" Vera tries for nonchalance as she picks up a second seashell. "Soon?"

"Not for a while. But the alarm is already set for a disconnection, so talking about it won't help. Are you ready?"

She nods.

"Throw!" Quarrels swings with the spinning shells and fires twice, splintering the first into five pieces, missing the double. No applause. Vera's smile remains but her eyes are glinting and cruel. "There's work I must do," he says. "I have a schedule to follow. Maybe I can arrange something next time so the Commission won't miss me. I know how to adjust the coordinates."

"Next time, no alarm?"

"I promise."

"And we'll be together forever?"

"I promise, my darling."

Y41-AK9 complains to his Auditor: If the System is just, why does it permit injustice?

What would you suggest?

Authorization by Center Control for the immediate apprehension of the subject. The necessary equipment could be delivered by Sentinel.

It is not the duty of the Depository to police the world.

But who else is to do it? The Law Speakers take no action. Itubi is given shelter wherever he goes. A female is housing him now. He has a life of ease ahead. Is that just? If the residents of Level I ever guess his fate, there will be complete chaos.

Center Control Regulations specify that the goal of Level I is acceptance of the Depository as their only world. Residents must learn to have faith in the System. Knowledge of truth is a precious responsibility, Y41-AK9. Perhaps continued exposure to the outside is weakening your trust. Temptations are strongest when Intellect and Ego cloud the mind.

I strive for patience and wisdom.

We suggest it. Without those qualities delusions arise, rash recommendations not congruent with order are seriously offered, the oblique workings of the subconscious revealed. To propose using machines against man is absurd; to imply that an Auditor might break his vows and pass along forbidden information to a lower-level resident is unimaginable. If performance of duty is proving too heavy a burden for Y41-AK9, then perhaps another Auditor can be assigned to the Subject.

My endeavors will be doubled with the wise assistance of those who see farther and guide me when I go astray.

The Weaver's palm-thatched house stands on the crest of a hill overlooking the sea. Gaudy jungle fowl scratch in the yard in front of the open door. Itubi sits on the step, mending a wooden stool, surrounded by the geometric patterns boldly painted on the whitewashed cut-coral walls. Skeins of newly dyed yarn hang in brilliant loops from the drying racks above his head, an awning as bright and ever changing as a rainbow. Everywhere he looks, he is confronted by color. Even the vegetable plots are divided by opulent rows of flowers.

He closes his eyes and listens to the sounds of the shuttle as Oona works at her loom inside. While he is prone to sit and dream, Oona is never idle—tending the dyeing vats, sweeping, drawing water from the cistern, spinning cotton fiber into yarn at her wheel, working in the garden. Her chores begin at sunrise and end in the smoky flickering light of a beeswax candle. She never asks his help, and except for two days a week when he leads the horse along the coastal path to the broad central valley and returns with a bale of cotton strapped to the pack saddle, Itubi is forced to invent work, finding simple tasks like the wobbling stool to fill his day. Aside from some desultory whittling, he has made no attempt to sculpt. The urge is no longer in him.

Still, Obu is content. Life is pleasant and warm. The bee-hives hum like a row of dynamos behind the house. Slender green lizards scramble in and out of the garden wall. A flame-crested jungle cock chases a chattering hen across the yard. Oona sings inside the house. "I am better than a roos-ter," Itubi muses. "The woman is pleased with me. Not a night without lovemaking. Should I be blamed if she has no other use for my arms?"

The loom is silent. Soon Oona appears in the doorway, carrying a round loaf of bread and a basket piled with fruit, wedges of goat cheese, a shattered coconut, and fat oozing squares of honeycomb. She sits, placing the basket between them on the step, and slices the loaf into broad slabs with a bone-handled knife. As always, she is smiling.

Obu spreads honey on the dark bread. "You seem happy today," he says.

"I am happy every day." Oona peels an orange. "But today there is special cause for joy."

"I could tell. I've never heard you sing before."

"The song should be yours as well, Obu. Your seed is alive within me. Today is my time of the month, and yet my menses do not flow. I'm pregnant, Obu."

"Impossible!"

"I knew it from our first union. You should rejoice."

"It's not true. I'm sterile, you know that. All male fetuses are sterilized in the hatchery, that's the law." Itubi feels his heartbeat accelerate. He wipes a smear of honey off his chin.

"What law, Obu?"

"Why, World Council law, to prevent unauthorized breeding and ensure . . ." Itubi falters. The old schoolboy slogans implanted hypnotically in his memory are of no help. Oona must know them all: MOTHERHOOD IS A PRIVILEGE, NOT A RIGHT. CONTROLLED POPULATION IS THE KEY TO WORLD PEACE. STERILITY EQUALS STABILITY. They were as much a part of childhood as the Mother Goose doggerel that returns to nag at him from out of the past:

> Born in a hatchery,
> Without the help of mother;
> That's the reason why I'm me
> And all the world's my brother!

Oona reaches across to grip his trembling hand. "You are your own authority now, Obu," she says.

"I'm sorry, my head is full of nursery rhymes. I forgot where I am, or even who I am. There no longer is any World Council, is there?"

"Not since the Awakening."

"And you're really going to have a baby?"

"Of course."

"There's no law forbidding it?"

"Nothing is forbidden. The Law Speakers provide guidance for the tribe, not restrictions."

"Incredible!"

Itubi remembers the complex procedure of obtaining his first child: the application forms, the psychiatric interviews and medical examinations, the long appraisal period, all the restrictions and redtape he and his wife submitted to before the hatchery approved their request. And even after an infant was reserved in their name on the production schedule, the complications continued. There were parental guidance clinics, mandatory infant care classes, a series of injections for his wife to induce lactation. PARENTHOOD MEANS RESPONSIBILITY!

"No, I don't believe it," he says. "You're making it up. My wife never menstruated. Females were fixed in the hatcheries just like the men."

"All but one in every thousand, Obu."

"That's right, all but the bleeders."

"Obu, I was a . . . *bleeder.* Those cruel slang words hurt when I was a girl. It was not an easy life being an Ovulator. Normal people didn't understand. I was medicated for eleven years, one thousand units of TCG every two weeks, and every month in the Incubation Center of Brazil Hatchery Twenty my uterus was drained by a suction tube. Once my yield was one hundred and seventy-three eggs."

"What about the Depository?"

"I was never in the Depository. Listen, eleven years was enough. This island was a holiday retreat in the old days; there was no permanent population. I made it look like an accident, ditched my gyro-gravcraft in the sea. When the other tourists were recalled after the Awakening, I hid in the forest. I never knew what it was all about. For ten years, maybe more, life was easy; food is no problem here. Then they started coming back, the ones from the Depository, and I spied on them until I learned enough to mingle without notice. I just appeared one day after a ship sailed and was accepted without question."

"Where did you learn to weave?"

"At the State Handicraft Preservation Center in Rio. Government Ovulators had lots of free time. We were encouraged to take up hobbies, you know, for extra points on our credit ratings."

"Did you really escape? It seems impossible. When were you born?"

"Sagittarius, twenty-one sixty."

"I'm just four years older." Itubi laughs. "Part of me anyhow. Yet you look so young, Oona."

"The final hatchery lifespan estimates were for five hundred to six hundred years."

"But, I've seen old men—"

"I know. Some of them from the Depository wither and die within a decade of getting out. Spend all their time fasting and praying. I've watched hundreds. No one seems to care. By living alone I escape close attention. These new Depository products are not suspicious of solitude as long as you act industrious or spiritual."

"Are there no others like us?"

"I've looked, and waited . . . nearly two hundred years. In all that time, you're the first. The ones that return from the Depository are sexless. Not their bodies, of course, they all have fine healthy hatchery bodies. Something's been done to their minds."

"Liberation," Itubi mutters.

"But you weren't Liberated. You're the runaway." Oona smiles, pleased with the thought of Itubi evading the machines. "You're famous. I heard all about you in the village before . . . before we met. I knew you were different, but I never, never guessed that you'd be fertile. The Breeding Facility must wait for the final operation to sterilize the males."

"Then it's just an accident. Swann's oversight." Itubi shakes his head. "Can it really be so simple?"

"There is nothing more simple than life, Obu," she says. "Miracles included."

Vera spreads an even film of coconut oil across Philip's back.

Her smile congeals when the electric buzz of his wrist alarm interrupts the placid afternoon. She caps the bottle, wiping her hands on the towel without a word.

"I'm sorry," Quarrels says, propped on his elbows. "It couldn't be helped." He avoids her eyes. "I know I gave my word, but it's not as easy as all that. God knows how many regulations I'm breaking by just being here."

"You're not going," she says.

"I have to. Next time it will be different."

"Never mind next time! You're not going." She drops the towel and walks quickly up the beach toward the tent. Quarrels watches her disappear inside and makes up his mind. This is the end. No more lies or compromises; he is tired of subterfuge and considers applying for therapy sessions to strengthen his resolve. All dreams must end in waking, he thinks, standing up as Vera comes out of the tent carrying the double-barreled Holland & Holland.

"Turn it off," she commands. "Whatever it is that you do, *do it!*"

"It's automatic, Vera. The controls are set back in the Depository."

"I don't believe you." She stops a few paces away in the sand and aims the shotgun at his face. "I mean it, I'll kill you if you don't turn it off."

Quarrels laughs. He looks straight into the upturned muzzle. Vera's eyes are no less threatening. "Such cheap Hollywood theatrics," he says. "You can't kill me, Vera. This is only a merge; it's as unreal as the movies. You can't do in memory what you haven't done in life."

"But it's true, I killed a man, my first husband. With this same gun. It's as easy as turning off your alarm. Now hurry up or I pull the trigger!"

"I believe you would, Vera, but it's still no good, even if you have a dozen victims to your credit. You may be a killer, but I've never been killed, so your threats are meaningless."

"I'm warning you, Philip." As she speaks, a mysterious light begins to play on his skin. "Philip!" The light flickers like little tongues of blue flame. *"Turn it off!"*

"Goodbye, Vera." The entire surface of his body is lambent. Radiance begins to blur his features. "I applaud your performance."

"Stay with me," she pleads. *"Please!"* The light is incredibly bright. Vera's scream is lost in the roar of the shotgun's blast.

Tauriq the Healer receives Oona's astonishing news calmly. Only his eyes betray his momentary amazement. He takes both her hands in his grasp and returns her steady gaze. For a long time neither speaks.

"And what of the stranger?" Tauriq asks, breaking the silence.

"Obu," Oona corrects him.

"Yes, Obu. Does he share your happiness and peace?"

"No, his Ego is too strong. His pride gives him no rest."

"I met him once in the village. His hostility is unmistakable. And yet, I sensed something vital in him, a life force more beast than man. I understand how it must have happened, Oona."

The Weaver laughs. "You sound as if I have a disease, Tauriq," she says.

"Perhaps it is even more serious than that. How long has it been?"

"Two months."

"It's time I had a look at you." Tauriq opens his shoulderbag and sorts among his instruments. "I've helped many mares to foal, but this will be my first childbirth." He removes a steel speculum and adjusts the calibrated spreaders.

Oona slips out of her loose cotton clothing, standing naked in front of the Healer. Above their heads, broad orange sunflowers nod in the afternoon wind.

Obu Itubi is drunk. He stumbles down the jungle trail, cursing the shifting weight of a sackful of avocados slung over his shoulder. What sort of work is this for a man who's fathered the world's first child in a hundred and fifty years? No, longer than that. The Reproduction Centers were started three centuries ago. Nothing but hatchery babies in all that time and he, a man as important as Adam, is sent to pick fruit in the forest like some paltry menial.

It's the woman's fault, with her loom and her house and that damned garden. The beatific Weaver! Well, he's had enough of being a lackey, running her errands. And for what? Cast-off clothing and tasteless vegetarian meals! Obu trudges forward, his beer-blurred brain tabulating a long list of complaints and injuries, not the least of which is the cooling of Oona's passion. She hasn't shared her bed with him since telling him she was pregnant a month ago, acting chaste as a vestal nun whenever he chances a caress. One would think she's harboring an immaculate conception in that proud stomach. But he remembers how she sweated and scratched and screamed his name in the night, damned if she didn't. And he'll be damned if another night goes by without the hump and thrust of love. No more sleeping in a hammock outside, as if he was no better than the goats she keeps. Some goat! Why, he's the mightiest ram in all the world.

Itubi staggers out of the woods, delighting in his newly discovered goathood. Yessir, the Universal Ram! He laughs and cavorts, swinging the sack in a wild circle that sends him spinning off his feet into the tall grass. Why wait for nighttime for his tupping? Oona's farm is just over the next hill. Why not sneak around the back way and take her by surprise, like he did the first time? A proper goat plan.

Itubi abandons the sack of avocados. They'll keep until he returns. Emboldened by alcohol, laughing his hircine laugh, he lopes through the waving grass, a copper-colored satyr all musk and gonad. What luck, finding the fallen-down remains of his lean-to under the pear trees, his brewpot still full and fermenting. Sober, he might have second thoughts about so rash an enterprise as rape, but strong drink happily obscures any lingering scruples and keeps the fantasy lamp of courage in full flame.

At the stone wall enclosing the upper meadow, Itubi drops to his knees and crawls, hidden from view until he reaches the barn. From here it's a short run to the house. He peers around the corner and sees Oona with another man, her clothing discarded at her feet. The stranger fondles her naked breasts. He whispers secret words into her ear. She is laughing as she reclines on a bench under the brazen sunflowers. Still laughing, she spreads her legs. The wicked-looking speculum gleams in his hands.

Itubi steps inside the barn, desperate and reeling. The sound of Oona's laughter goads his fury. A row of wooden tools hang from pegs driven into the stone wall, a lethal array of scythes, grubbing hoes, hay forks, and rakes. It takes only a moment for him to make his choice. Gripping the long-handled flail like a club, Itubi starts from the barn, his bare feet cat-silent on the packed earth of the farmyard. The stranger is bending over his woman, savoring the delights of those open thighs. He doesn't hear Itubi's approach or see the fleeting shadow of the upraised flail as he poises to strike.

Vera hurls the shotgun aside and hurries to where her lover's body lies sprawled in the sand. She knows he is dead and the moment of horror she felt while pulling the trigger is gone, replaced by a curious calm. There is no grief, not even the beginnings of guilt. She is troubled only by the sharp echo of the weapon's report still ringing in her ears. A sense of awe at having caused such terrifying damage is as near as she comes to true emotion.

Because the range was too close for the pattern to spread, Quarrels took the full charge straight into his face. He lies on his back, arms spread, his head burst like an overripe melon carelessly dropped in the field. Vera is astonished by the quantity of blood puddled in the warm sand. The foxfire phosphorescence no longer emanates from his body and, in spite of the suntan, his flesh assumes a ghastly pallor.

"Dead fish only glow at night," Vera mutters, kicking sand at the fat bluebottle flies that have appeared almost magically about the corpse. Quarrels is hers forever now. He will never go away again.

A man's life is his own if he causes no harm to others. The Law Speaker's recorded words issue from within the Sentinel. All the Elders of the Qaf tribe have gathered in the Weaver's garden, summoned by the flying silver robot towering above their heads. The cloth-draped form of Tauriq the

Healer rests on a bench under the sunflowers. One of the Law Speakers holds the bloodstained flail. Oona stands, watching silently, off to the side.

"There is no need for such reminders," the Law Speaker says. "I recall the words I spoke."

My apologies, Enlightened One, Y41-AK9 replies via communicator. *I do not wish to dishonor you, nor do I care to use this sorrowful occasion to further my own wishes.*

"We are in your debt for bringing us here. Your warnings might have prevented this loss. The fugitive must be returned to the Depository. He cannot escape from the island. All of the tribe will assist you in the search."

He is more dangerous than any animal. Care must be taken so that no harm comes to your people.

"All caution will be exercised. We employ nets and darts tipped with a paralyzing anesthetic. Our hunters are extremely accurate with the blowgun. The runaway will be captured alive."

If it can be managed, the Depository will be grateful. The Sentinel contains cranial facilities adapted specifically for the return of the resident. But, if the lives of any of your men are endangered, it is the wish of Center Control that the subject be destroyed.

The Medical Authority is puzzled. In all their records there is not another case like this one. A Level II Auditor, the only resident of that category born in the twentieth century, is the subject. His medical history file reads:

Number:	C19-LTR85 (266-07-83)
Name:	Philip Randolph Quarrels
Sex:	Male
Class:	not applicable
Born:	8-19-1940
Cerebrectomized:	3-23-1990
Filed:	10-10-2362
Occupation:	Astronaut; pilot
Ego Rating:	67.459
Health:	Excellent
Previous Illness:	None

The Medical Authority is notified after the subject failed to meet his auditing schedule and did not respond when signaled via communicator.

The resident's brain is currently undergoing intense laboratory examination. Although tests indicate that the cerebral cell tissue is alive and the neurons respond to electrostimuli, no wave patterns can be detected on the micro-encephalogram. Even in the deepest of comas the subconscious still emits a feeble pattern. Clinically, the subject is alive; and yet, according to all known diagnoses, the brain is that of a dead man.

It is very mysterious. No trace of disease or cell damage can be found. No symptoms of psychic trauma are discovered. A playback of the subject's files reveals nothing. Previous to the discovery of the subject's condition he had programmed a series of memory-bank epistemology lectures. Curiously, nothing of the content of these lectures has registered in the conscious or unconscious mind of the subject. It is almost as if he had been someplace else when the files were programmed. Center Control has instructed the Medical Authority to continue its investigations.

Obu Itubi cowers in an impromptu burrow he scooped from the hillside with his bare hands. He is raw and dirty, his hair matted and caked with clay. The cuts and scratches from scrambling blindly through thorn-sharp jungle undergrowth have begun to fester. Ticks and lice torment him. It is damp in the burrow and Itubi is cold, cramped, and utterly miserable.

He hasn't eaten in two days. To avoid observation, his plan was to forage for food only at night, but, without a moon, the darkness under the trees was like a bandage tied over his eyes and it was all he could do to feel his way back to the safety of his burrow, a helpless hungry mole. He tries not to think of Oona or of his comfortable life in the whitewashed house. Regret is an insidious poison and Itubi has need of memories considerably less toxic than the image of the slender Tropique weaver who carries his child in her

sloping belly. He concentrates his thoughts on the monotonous aisles of the Depository and determines to appreciate
even what harried freedom is left to him. Better to live in the
ground like a cornered rat and die a free man under the open
sky than be sealed away in that computerized mausoleum
with several billion other zombies.

Sustained by his angry thoughts, Itubi has no intention of
dying. Killing an innocent man may have cost him a chance
for domestic happiness, but as long as he has the strength to
resist, he is not going to give up his freedom because of a
drunken mistake. Itubi knows that he is not safe on the
island. Escape means stealing a boat and for such an under-
taking he needs nourishment. The risks of starvation are
greater than the danger of exposing himself. If he's cautious,
an hour's foraging should enable him to stockpile enough
fruit to last for days.

Itubi pushes past the leaves and branches which camouflage his dugout, stretching his aching limbs for the first
time since the previous night. He savors the warm sunlight
on his skin and starts stiff-legged through the waist-high
foliage. There is not a sound in the forest. Even the raucous
jungle birds are silent. Itubi is certain he's alone and unob-
served. His thoughts of security are interrupted by his own
startled outcry. A sudden searing pain, more virulent than
any wasp's sting, burns across his shoulder. Grimacing, Itubi
reaches behind to feel the barbed shaft hanging from his

flesh. Before he can pull it out, his knees buckle and he drops forward into darkness.

Philip Quarrels is buried without ceremony. Using an empty coconut shell, Vera scrapes a shallow pit in the sand. Chi-Chi is employed to move the corpse. A rope attached to a makeshift harness is tied to the dead man's feet and the horse drags the body to the open grave, leaving a smooth trail across the beach like the track of an ovulating sea turtle. There are no prayers or obsequies. Vera rolls him in and covers him up.

Altogether, Vera spends considerably more time decorating the grave than she did preparing it. She pats the sand smooth in a high mound over the pit. Around the perimeter she arranges a row of queen conch shells, bleached white by the sun. In a second row, the shells are upside down to reveal the pink involute openings. Elsewhere, fragile slivers of the shattered lime skeletons of sea urchins are pressed into the mound in an abstract mosaic.

Vera is pleased with the result. She has arranged the grave so it can be seen through the open flap of her tent. Every day she will bring baskets of flowers and strew them over the mound. Down the beach she knows where to find a large lump of brain coral that will make a suitably ironic headstone. Vera looks forward to the histrionics of mourning. It will give her something to help pass the time.

Attention, B-0489 . . . Attention . . .

Obu Itubi recognizes the presence of his Auditor on the communicator. This is puzzling. He remembers leaving the dugout and the stillness of the forest, but everything else is vague, lost in blackness.

Attention, attention, B-0489. There is no point in playing mute, we know you are receiving this transmission.

Where am I?

Safely back in the bosom of Center Control. You will excuse me for being less precise, but the exact location would be meaningless to you.

What has happened to my body?

It was incinerated on Antilles Nine. You were cerebrectomized by a Healer there, a colleague of your unfortunate victim.

And what will happen to me now?

Your most interesting question, B-0489 . . .

I know I am at your mercy.

Very true. And since you showed so little of that commodity during your rampage in the Surface Installation, I imagine you feel a bit apprehensive.

I'm not afraid. There's nothing more you can do to me.

You display your ignorance, B-0489. Center Control has on file pain so profound that your imagination cannot even begin to fathom the potential agony. We can condemn you to eternal purgatory by merely flipping a switch.

Do it then.

You are too impetuous, B-0489. That's why you are so dangerous. Center Control has no desire for revenge. In spite of all provocation, I have not the slightest interest in "skewering you like a shish kebab."

So, you know all my secret thoughts. I should have expected as much.

Your mistake was in having thoughts which needed to be kept secret. Center Control records the complete consciousness of every resident. There is no such thing as secret thoughts. Even your unconscious is on file. My mistake was in not making a daily audit. If I had, perhaps all this destruction might have been avoided.

You've been brainwashed by the System. The machines have tricked you out of more than your body; they've stolen your mind as well.

There is no such thing as individual mind, B-0489, there is only the One Mind. All else is illusion. But I won't trouble you with further discourse on the Doctrine. You asked about your fate. I have been instructed by Center Control to inform you of their decision. As a result of your destructive actions, the brain of a Level I resident has been damaged beyond the possibilities of reconstruction. Although humanoid hatching and breeding facilities are maintained, the specimens produced have only a modified brain, so there is no chance of our laboratories supplying a replacement.

Because of this fact, Center Control has ordered that your brain, B-0489, be substituted for the one destroyed. All of your thoughts, both conscious and unconscious, will be erased and the files of the other resident substituted.

So, you mean to kill me after all?

Not exactly; your files will be consigned to the Archives for storage until such time as another brain is available. In effect, B-0489, you are to be placed in limbo. Before I end transmission, you might be interested in knowing of the metaphysical debate your case has occasioned. Center Control is undecided what the karmic results would be if your files were erased instead of placed in storage. Would erasure equal death, and thus a new incarnation for you on another world? Or would you simply be cast adrift in the samsara forever, doomed to an eternity of illusion? You might well use your final moments to meditate on this question, B-0489. Neuron purgation procedures will begin immediately.

End transmission.

CLICK.

Oona the Weaver sits in the sunshine of her garden, staring down past the green cultivated rows to the sea. A vibrancy of hummingbirds embellishes the flowerbeds; bees drone in the golden afternoon; a rooster struts and crows, parading his plumage along the top of the stone wall. Behind her in the house, her loom stands idle. Recently a vague dreaminess has overtaken her and she has done no work in days, sitting instead for hours in the garden, her hands folded in her lap.

Oona's smile is peaceful and contented. There, she feels it again, for the third time today. She lifts her hands to the swollen sides of her stomach and feels the quickening within her body. She thinks of the tiny fetus, already perfectly formed, kicking out his unborn legs, restless with the novelty of life. Her joy is complete.

An Amco-pak Mark II moves silently between the narrow steel shelves in the Archives. Ranked along either side are endless file containers, catalogued and forgotten in the mortuary stillness. Clamped in his telescoping arms, the file machine carries the complete files of resident Obu Itubi. The square metal container is identified only by number: B-0489-M(773-22-99). After a moment's scanning, the Mark II finds the appropriate shelf and slides the files into place. The aisle is too narrow to turn around, so the scanner turret pivots 180 degrees, the controls are set on reverse, and the machine backs smoothly out the way it came. On another shelf, two rows over, sit the files containing information on the whereabouts of a twentieth-century resident (female), the lost key to Vera Mitlovic's freedom.

A reconstituted Skeets Kalbfleischer is having a nightmare. Although this dream has occurred with increasing regularity over the past weeks, Skeets has yet to report the details to Y41-AK9, his new Auditor. It is always the same room, brilliantly hung with Sung dynasty scrolls and tapestries. The Emperor is always there, supervising from his teakwood throne, a slightly mocking smile playing about his thin lips. Skeets is strapped to the top of a porcelain-tiled table. As before, he is in a strange body: adult, well muscled, with copper-colored skin and a shock of fine coal-black hair.

The Emperor claps his hands and the torture begins. Three men enter the room, two of them pushing a brass-bound cabinet exquisitely fitted with dozens of tiny drawers. These two men assist the surgeon in selecting the proper instruments from the cabinet. A large mirror hangs over the table so Skeets can watch each detail of the operation. The surgeon works with skilled fingers, diligently removing tiny portions of flesh from his body. Each incision is in a different place. One cut removes a portion of earlobe, another takes the tip off his big toe. The surgeon is a master of his ancient craft; under his patient care a victim is kept alive for days as, bit by bit, his body is carved away. First, the skin is removed; next, the flayed muscles minutely diced. By avoiding vital organs, the surgeon whittles the body down to bones and guts, never allowing any one cut to induce shock or trauma.

Although the pain is constant and unvarying, the victim is never allowed to lose consciousness.

Skeets watches the entire process; his eyelids were the first to go, thereby ensuring his unswerving attention. But even after his eyes are removed and he is reduced to a beating heart, a single lung, and the blanched stalk and blossom of spinal column and skull, Skeets is still able to witness the final moments of his dream. He sees it all in the mirror as clearly as if he still had eyes. One of the attendants produces a fine silver saw from an appropriately shaped drawer. With a few swift strokes, the surgeon uncaps the cranium and eases the brain out of its ivory nest. Gray and glistening, the wrinkled lump of nervous tissue is carried to the Emperor on a golden dish with the polite hope that it will please his discriminating palate.